The Dead Shall March

Tim Callanan

Michael Terence
Publishing

First published in paperback by
Michael Terence Publishing in 2020
www.mtp.agency

ISBN 9781800940352

Cover design
2020 Michael Terence Publishing

To my grandparents, Dominick and Una,
for all their love and support.

Contents

Prologue

The Master and Apprentice stormed through the room, slaying the guards. The Master walked over to the crystal ball while the Apprentice dealt with the remaining soldiers. They had repeated this so many times before. They knew what they were doing.

The Apprentice strode over to the only human in the room and put a sword to his throat.

“Please no,” the man begged. “I’m sorry for what I did. I’ll help you any way I can. Just please, please, don’t kill me. I don’t want to die. I never wanted it to go like this. Please, please-”

“Silence!” the Master roared. The man whimpered. “How long ago did he leave here?”

“Plcasc, plcasc-”

“How long ago!”

“Two years. Please, please-”

“Where?”

“I don’t know. Please, please, please-”

“Then you are of no further use to me and you will get what you deserve.”

With one swift stroke, the Master sent the man’s head rolling.

“Two years? We are getting close,” the Apprentice remarked.

He walked over to the large glass window built into one side of the tower. From there, he could see the whole city, knowing that chaos would engulf it after they were finished here. He smiled. Justice was coming.

"He left in a rush. He knows we are after him," the Master replied. "He didn't even finish this place, leaving this fool in charge and rebels still abroad. Aye, we are close."

He walked over to the ball and brought one side of his sword swiftly onto it, ending the creature's control of that place.

"We are coming for you, Diabolous."

1: The Riders

Alexander winced as his sword crashed from his hand yet again. He felt so frustrated. Bad enough to constantly lose but his opponent didn't even appear to be trying that hard to defeat him.

"I'm ready, Hyp," said Alex, seizing up his sword again and wielding it with all his strength.

Grinning, Hyperion launched into a fresh attack. Alex had no chance, he landed one hit before his opponent dashed his sword to the ground, sending up sparks as the metal struck the stone floor.

Alex had never liked sword fighting or any other sport for that matter. He had neither the strength nor the build. He was tall enough but with his fair hair and brown eyes, people often remarked on how closely he resembled his mother. He had always preferred reading books and studying maps to sports. But his father insisted. He had to keep up with practice once a week because the son of a duke must be able to fight if his people needed him. His elder brother Bruce excelled at everything and had huge physical prowess; compared to Alex he impressed all as a born leader. The people loved him and with good reason.

"Is that the best you can do, Al?"

Hyperion's skill with a sword beat Alex every time, even though he preferred to wield an axe. The two young men shared a loyal friendship. Hyperion served as a soldier in the palace guard, like his father and grandfather before him. He had grown up around the palace and as the same age as Alex, they naturally spent all their time together. Apart from the sword fighting, they enjoyed similar interests especially reading and learning history.

Just as Alex retrieved his sword from the floor and braced himself for another attack, a messenger ran into the yard.

"My Lord, his Grace requests your presence in the throne room."

"I finished beating you anyway," said Hyperion, smiling. "I have to go on duty soon. Maybe you'll do better next time."

Alex grinned ruefully then hurried away to change his clothes before attending the throne room. His father always insisted he looked respectable in his presence. The throne room had an awesome majesty, its massive walls illuminated by many windows positioned high above. Some people warned that this diminished the safety of the castle itself but with so many guards positioned around the perimeter, it had never posed a problem. Multiple doors on each side lead to various antechambers and corridors. Servants bustled around the room at all times but the authorities had no fear of spies infiltrating as the most important conversations took place behind locked and guarded doors. As well as the servants, important officials attended audiences with his Grace the Duke. Today, he had summoned only Alex and his brother, Bruce, along with a messenger from the Pass. The Duke looked up as Alex entered.

"Ah, Alexander."

"Father. You called for me?"

"I want you to hear this. Charles here has ridden from the Pass saying that a group from the Empire came through. Is that right?"

"Yes, Your Grace," replied the messenger. "They came through two days ago and should arrive here tomorrow. They bring disturbing news. I wanted to deliver it myself, rather than by bird, to make sure you understood the full of it. They confirmed the stories we have heard of horrific creatures raiding their villages. More than that, they say the Emperor is dead and the Capital has fallen."

"That doesn't make sense to me," said Bruce. "We have heard many stories of their Capital and their strong army. We have even fought them a few times, years ago and they were always close to defeating us. How can they suddenly fall down before mere raiding parties?"

"That will hopefully become clear when this group arrives," said his father. "Once we know that, we will take precautions to make sure it doesn't happen to us. You're all dismissed. Apart from you, Alexander. Let us talk for a while."

"I hear you are keeping up with your sword practice with Hyperion?" the Duke said, once the others had filed out of the room.

"Yes, father."

"That's good. I'm getting old, you know. It will need both you and your brother to rule this land if these stories are true. Once he takes the throne, you will have to step up and help him. He is strong but rash. Too much like me. Whereas you, you have the brains of my father. I hope you won't let me, or him, down."

"I give you my word, father."

"Go, then. I'm sure you have important things on hand, as do I."

Alexander left the throne room and headed back to his own room, thinking of the worrying new information. *Father is definitely feeling old,* he thought as he walked. He seemed to talk about it more and more these days, even though he still appeared strong. The other news, now that really did disturb Alex. He and Hyperion had read a lot about the Empire in various history books. If they had fallen to these creatures, what chance did his duchy stand? Even if the seven other duchies came to their aid, a terrible battle threatened. As soon as he reached his room, he began pulling out some old maps and books he had collected over the years.

By the time the riders reached the city the next day, practically all the citizens had heard the news, either from servants or the messenger. Crowds awaited them in the streets. The guards let the soldiers straight in, directed stable hands to take charge of their horses and escorted the exhausted men up to the palace. They had ridden for many days to get to the duchy. Some bore cuts and wounds, their clothes looked dirty and torn. They had to leave their weapons outside the throne room. Even though it had been a couple of decades since they had last been at war with the Empire and plenty of trade links had developed since then, the people still didn't trust the Empire's warriors with weapons.

When this dishevelled and weary group entered the throne room, they discovered a welcoming party comprising some of the most important authorities in the land. The Duke greeted them and introduced his sons, Bruce and Alexander, followed by Helena, wife of Bruce and captain of the city guard. General Tyson, in charge of the duchy's military aspects, stepped forward, together with Lord Marcus, the Duke's most trusted advisor, involved in all major decisions and never far from his side during meetings of the highest level. He was also the Duke's first cousin and served as a soldier in his younger days but had taken an arrow to the knee in combat which ended his military career.

Alex saw Hyperion standing guard at the door and they exchanged a quick grin. Then the leader of the group stepped forward.

"His Grace, the Duke of Cosando," announced the herald. "Welcomes Captain Theodore of the city guard of Impoarca."

"Your Grace, I bring you important news," said Captain Theodore, bowing. He was a tall man, dark-skinned, well-built, obviously a soldier of many years by his military bearing.

"Speak, then," the Duke replied. "For I have already heard part of your story and am keen to understand how it came about. So, begin your report."

"Well, sir, it began about a year and a half ago. Suddenly hundreds of immigrants tried to cross the Armary Mountains to the north of our Empire, bringing stories of war and destruction caused by vile monsters. At the time, we did not pay them much heed. And then, raids began happening on our towns nearest the mountains. We upped our forces and pushed them back as best as we could, killing many but sustaining losses.

"Two weeks ago, a messenger arrived at Impoarca with a hundred of the creatures at his back. We could have easily defeated them but they bore the white flag of truce with them. The messenger looked human and he had a huge helmet covering his face. He walked up to the gate and began talking to the soldiers on guard. I was one of them. He said "I bear a message from my Master. He says to surrender and live or be completely destroyed. What is your response to this fair request?" We dispatched a runner to the palace immediately and soon General Agordum himself came to the gate. He told the messenger we would never surrender and the messenger left.

"A couple of days' later I received the order to assemble a group of soldiers to bring you news of these creatures and ask for your support. Yet when we arrived at our outpost closest to the Pass, I heard that the Capital had fallen and the Emperor slain. The outpost had suffered multiple raids and only a small number of warriors survived. Lieutenant Felltear here served as the commanding officer at that outpost. I rounded up what soldiers remained and continued my journey here, to complete my final mission as commanded by the Emperor."

"You bring us disturbing news, Captain," said the Duke, after a moment of silence. "Have all the cities in the Empire fallen?"

"Most of them, sir. Those situated on the islands off the coast will last a while longer until the creatures learn how to use boats. The rest were still standing when we left but with the Capital gone and most of the army destroyed, they don't stand much of a chance."

"Neither, it would appear, do we," replied the Duke, darkly. "Now, describe these creatures to me."

"Sir, they are called goblins. From what we have seen, we think that they come in two types. The regular soldiers stand smaller than most men, around five feet tall. They use small daggers and swords. These are the most common, the others rarer. We think of them as the officers. When they appear, they take charge. They look taller than a full-grown man, something like eight feet in height. They use long spears with points at both ends. They are very strong in battle and can scare the ordinary goblins into doing anything. When led by one of these officers, normal goblins will never surrender no matter how outnumbered they are.

"The raiding parties come allied with cougars. These are giant mountain cats, very fast. They can outpace a horse on the flat and overcome any creature in the mountains. They have always lived high in the mountain passes but until now, they never came down from the mountains or attacked humans. Now, they roam the forests at will and have adapted to survive the woodland habitat as if they had always lived there. They attack unarmed humans on sight and can even defeat an individual soldier. Worse than that, they prowl in powerful packs that can defeat a whole squad of well-trained warriors. They can leap great distances and great heights and don't care who they kill."

"Is there no way to defeat this threat?" said the Duke, almost to himself, fearing that his entire army would fail to match these creatures in a head to head battle.

"None that we know of, sir."

"There is a way."

Every head in the room spun round to look at the man who had spoken. Lieutenant Felltear stepped forward. An eyepatch covered one eye and he bore many scars of battle. He slowly took in the gathered audience and when he suddenly smiled, Alexander felt a shiver run down his back.

"There is a way," he repeated.

"Tell us, then, if you know it," commanded the Duke.

"A couple of weeks back, the goblins captured me and my squad whilst out on patrol. Eventually, I managed to escape but my squad wasn't so lucky. While I was held, I overheard the goblins discussing their master's den and those who had visited it spoke of a crystal ball. They told the others that it was the source of all his power. If it represents such power to them, I think that if you were to destroy it, you would succeed in destroying him too."

"Intriguing," said the Duke. "Why were they talking about this?"

"It seemed like they were showing off to the other goblins, boasting about how much they knew. I noticed a constant struggle for power between the two groups. Each group of goblins thought they should be in charge. When they were talking about this, they thought we were all asleep."

"Are you sure this would work?" asked the Duke.

"No. But it seems to me it is your only choice. And I don't think the goblins had any reason to lie. "

"Very interesting." The Duke paused for a moment. "Thank you, Lieutenant Felltear. I think that's enough for now," he said, addressing the group of men. "You will be given food and shelter and may wander at will in the city but do not leave. We may have further use for you."

Captain Theodore and his men bowed and left the room.

"Alexander, Bruce, General Tyson come with me and Marcus," commanded the Duke as soon as the doors closed behind the group of men.

He led the way through a side door into an adjoining room. It was much smaller than the throne room. A large table stood at the centre and shelves filled with maps and old books lined the walls. A map of the Duchy of Cosando hung on the far wall. Alex had rarely seen this room, known to all as the War Room, a place to plan attacks and to decide how to defend the duchy. It had been used rarely in his father's reign, apart from when dealing with small attacks by barbarian tribes.

Marcus walked over to one of the shelves, selected a map and spread it on the table. Alex drew closer to look. It was a map of the Empire and the land north of the Empire, as far as beyond the Armary Mountains. They knew very little about this land. Few travellers braved it and no trade took place with the inhabitants and the people of Cosando. All they had heard was it comprised many small, warring countries, populated with tough and unfriendly citizens. However, Alex noticed that the map in front of him looked detailed, naming all the major cities and their rulers, names of lakes and the separate countries.

"Where did you get this?" Alex asked.

"We've had it for years," replied Marcus. "Throughout history men have wished to explore the unknown. One of them brought back a map during the reign of one of your ancestor's and they copied his information onto this. We don't know how accurate it is but now, this news proves it won't be of much use."

"Which brings us around to the point of this meeting," said the Duke. "How to deal with this threat?"

"Should we involve the other dukes in this discussion?" asked Bruce.

"No time," said Marcus "It would take over a week to call a meeting and even longer than that before a decision was made, with all the time it takes to get everyone to agree. No, we will decide ourselves and tell the others afterwards."

"So, any suggestions?" asked the Duke.

"It's simple," said Bruce. "We send a group over the mountains and destroy this ball of power."

"What if there is no ball? All we have to prove this is the report of a soldier we don't even know, overhearing goblins' talking about it," said Marcus.

"Then we kill the Master. It can't be that hard," persisted Bruce.

"No. It's too dangerous," countered Marcus.

"It may be our only option," said Tyson. "We will have to trust this information. The only other thing is to face them in open battle. And we all know what that would be like."

A silence descended as each of the four men pictured the lives that would cost only to result in certain defeat.

"If we send a group, it will have to be small," said Alex. "I mean, the only thing we can do is sneak in, not fight them in battle."

"He's right," said Marcus, after considering this. "Two dozen should be enough. A dozen of our soldiers and a dozen of those warriors from the Empire. We will need a strong leader. And the best warriors."

"I'll go," Bruce said immediately.

"No," said the Duke. "You are the heir. Your place is here, with your people."

"There will be no people if we fail in this. Besides, Al can do just fine while I'm away. Marcus said best warriors. That's me and General Tyson and he can't go because he is our general and our expert at fighting wars."

"I agree with Bruce," said Marcus. "He should go. He is our best option."

"What about Helena?" asked the Duke.

"She should come too," said Bruce. "You know she is almost as good as me. Plus, she is a captain of the guard and our soldiers will follow her anywhere."

"It still seems too risky. We don't know what it will be like. You will be walking through a warzone with only twenty-three other warriors. There could be thousands of goblins just waiting for you," said the Duke.

"It's a risk we will have to take," said Tyson. "Unless anyone can think of something, this is what must be done. And must be done soon. The longer we wait, the closer an enemy horde gets to our land, and our people."

"Well, if you must, you will leave in two days," said the Duke. "I will ask Captain Theodore to pick a dozen troops. The rest of his can go where they want to. That's only if he agrees to this plan. You're dismissed."

Alex and Bruce left, heading to the Old Hall. It was a place they always used to go as children. It hadn't been in official use for centuries, not since the newer hall was built. It was quite small and served a purpose only at the outset of the duchy. Alex loved it because no-one ever bothered them there. It was a place they could be alone and play, or, as they got older, a place to talk in private. Only he, Bruce and Hyperion ever went there.

"I don't like this, Bruce," said Alex, as they took up their accustomed seats in the Hall. "What if you fail? Or die?"

"Me? Fail? Die? Nah, you must be thinking of someone else," Bruce replied. "I could hardly leave you here, running the kingdom. But seriously, Al, it won't go badly."

"But-"

"It won't, Al. It sounds like a pretty easy job. I mean, even you could probably do it."

"What if-"

"None of your what-ifs, it'll be fine. We'll only be gone a couple of weeks and then it will be back to normal. Now, however, it's time to go," said Bruce, standing up. "You should go to training, being in charge now and all and I have preparations to attend to." He walked past Alex and patted him on the back. "It'll be fine. You'll see."

Alex and Bruce left the Hall, going their separate ways. Alex spent the rest of the day practising, now that it looked like they could be at war. They needed to begin training more troops in case Bruce failed and they had a battle on their hands. If that happened, Alex would have to lead troops into battle and he needed to prepare himself for this. He knew Hyperion was on duty most of the day so he'd have to find a different sparring partner. Bruce had to spend the day selecting his squad and planning for the journey.

2: The Capital

Alexander positioned himself up on the gate to watch his brother's group leave. Bruce had spent the entire day before with Helena, Marcus and Captain Theodore in the war room looking at maps and making plans. Alex had spent the day with his father and General Tyson, preparing plans in case of a goblin invasion. He also had to write a letter to the other dukes explaining the current situation. The messengers had left early that morning.

"Ah, our ferocious warriors prepare to set off!"

Alex turned around to see Father Zeno walking towards him, the High Priest of the duchy. Alex had never liked him much as he put all his faith in the Gods and not enough in people. But other than that, he seemed quite agreeable.

"Let us pray that the Gods grant them a safe journey and a successful mission."

"We can hope," said Alex, turning back to watch Bruce and Theodore gathering their riders.

Zeno hadn't dressed in his full ceremonial regalia today, just a plain blue robe. Blue was the prominent colour, except for ceremonial attire, because as well as High Priest, he was a priest of the Sky. He had also left his high hat behind, though he still held the long staff.

"Sadly, I fear where they are going the Gods cannot help."

"What?" Alex was surprised. He had never known the High Priest to doubt the Gods' power in anything. This was very unlike him. "Don't you always say the Gods control everything?"

"Aye, I do say that. But this feels different. Something is wrong. These creatures, these goblins, they sound like creatures of the darkness. I am a learned man in most of the affairs of the Gods and on many other matters but these sound like nothing from any of our books that I have read on them. So, after hearing the news, I searched through the dark book."

Alex gasped. He had heard tales of the dark book. It told terrifying stories, all about the thirteenth God, called the Abominable Power. No one spoke his real name, it wasn't even written down in the dark book and over the years it had been forgotten, if it had ever been known in the first place. Reading the dark book was forbidden. It was said that even being near it for too long could turn the best priests dark and evil. It was locked in a secure room underneath the temple. No-one knew why they had it, it had always been there as well as the other six texts.

"Yes, lad, I know what you're thinking," said Zeno, after seeing Alex's face. "But I had to. The other six texts contained nothing on these creatures. But the dark book described them the same as Captain Theodore did. They are His servants."

"You don't think He's here, do you?" Alex shuddered at the thought.

"No, lad. Definitely not. If these are truly His then it is just one of His captains leading them. Still powerful, I grant you, but they are fallible and if what the Lieutenant said is true, this is a weak one. Lord Bruce should have no trouble."

"I hope you're right," said Alex as he watched the group set out on their horses, then turned back and went inside, leaving Zeno still looking into the distance from the top of the wall.

Three days later, Bruce pushed forward through the Pass and into the warzone. The twenty-four warriors rode hard during each day and set up camp each night. Once through the Pass, they had to keep guard each night and ride more carefully during the day. They saw no goblin raiding parties.

A day out from the Pass, they encountered their first village by the road. They searched the houses for people or any goods. Nothing. Everywhere had been ransacked, everything broken or destroyed. Some buildings had been set on fire and blood flowed everywhere. In the centre of the village, they came across a pile of burnt skeletons, all that was left of the villagers. None had been spared from the flames. They also noted a couple of goblin corpses scattered around.

"My Gods," whispered Bruce.

"It was a massacre," said Helena. "They had no chance. There was no mercy."

"This is how they work," said Theodore. "No survivors. The whole Empire is like this now. That is why we must stop this. They have no use for humans, other than for sport. Men, women, children; they kill them all."

"Let's get out of here," said Bruce.

Six days later, they approached the Capital. They had passed a couple more towns and villages, all looking the same as the first. So far, they had encountered no goblins. Impoarca loomed in front of them, the largest city south of the Armary Mountains and built where the main trade road intersected a river. It was a city founded by traders centuries ago and far bigger than any Bruce or Helena had ever seen; it seemed to cover the whole horizon. The buildings looked massive compared to those in Cosando, where few buildings rose above two storeys. Here, some towered to five or six. It was rumoured to have a population of over a million, both military and civilians.

And it was dead.

No sound emanated from its streets. No lights shone. Nothing moved. It looked totally empty. Even from this distance, they could see some of the damage done to the buildings.

"Ah, the once magnificent Impoarca, capital of our great Empire. Now, it is nothing more than an empty pile of rubble," said Theodore, riding forward again.

"We shouldn't go in there," said Bruce. "Who knows how many goblins that city could contain. We should go around."

"We can't," replied Theodore. "There is no other bridge anywhere near here. It would take days to find a crossing and get back to the road on the other side; even then the bridges may be held against us or broken. No, I'd rather take our chances here. They have to have kept at least one bridge to use."

"Alright, then. But everyone, get ready. We could be attacked at any time. Theodore, you take the lead. You know the city."

Theodore pulled out his sword and shield and started forward. Bruce and Helena each pulled out two short swords and followed him. The rest of the soldiers brandished their assorted weapons and went forward with Felltear taking the rear. They approached the gate.

***

Alexander rode out to the Pass a couple of days after Bruce had set out. General Tyson went with him. Alex had always liked Tyson. He had risen quickly through the ranks of the army and had become general at only thirty. He had read quite a lot of history books, studying different tactics and when to use them. That was mainly why Alex liked him. Alex had always been fascinated by history during his school years and hadn't found many people around the castle he could have discussions with. Tyson had always been the most fun to talk to and had taught Alex and Hyperion many history lessons. On top of that, he was a great fighter and would've gone with Bruce if he didn't have obligations here. Bruce didn't like to admit it but Tyson could beat him in a duel with any type of weapon.

"Ah, the Pass of Titus," said Tyson as they approached. "Where Duke Titus, your grandfather, made his famous last stand to hold out the Empire's grand army. That was just after the last king was killed."

"Yes, I know. You've told me the story so many times," said Alex. "How he and his small army withstood wave after wave of enemies, waiting for reinforcements to come. And when they did come, they brought the news that the other dukes had executed the King because he had refused to fight the Empire and was going to surrender. My grandfather never left the front line and died later with three arrows stuck in him. He succeeded in holding out the enemy army and eventually the Empire had to retreat."

"Ah, so you were listening to me during those lessons. Alright then, if you know it all, what was the Pass called before his great feat?"

"Easy. It didn't really have a name but was just known as the Mountain Pass."

"Right. Not very creative, was it? And who was the leader of the other army?"

"General Xavier. Grandfather slew him himself, just before he died."

"Good."

They entered the small fortress at the Pass. Tyson gathered the warriors together and drilled them to test how proficient their training was. Tyson always checked with the soldiers to make sure they hadn't become sloppy in the years of mostly peace. With the threat of an invasion now likely, the Duke had decided to step up the defences at the Pass. They would improve fortifications as well as increasing the number of troops stationed there. Tyson had been sent to see to these preparations and Alex had been sent too to learn more about the defence of the Duchy. With Bruce gone, and his father too old, Alex would be expected to be on the battlefield when the fighting began. If it began. All over the Duchy, more soldiers were being trained up. Everyone was expected to help out to protect their homes and their families.

Alex climbed to the top of the fortress, thinking of all the knowledge and the tactics he had learnt over the last couple of days in preparation for the expected war to come. He had had practice every morning and meetings with Tyson and Lord Marcus most afternoons. He looked out through the Pass. *Don't fail, Bruce,* he thought pleadingly. *And please don't die.*

***

Bruce looked at the gates of Impoarca as they rode slowly past. They had suffered severe damage by a battering ram before being torn off their hinges. The guardhouse on the inside of the gate was completely destroyed and dead bodies littered the street. They had never got around to gathering and burning them. The sewers still ran red.

The horses walked slowly down the main street. Eight soldiers in the middle of the group had bows and arrows at the ready. No sound could be heard apart from the hooves on the cobbles and the quiet rushing of the river up ahead. No-one spoke. Theodore held up a hand for them to halt as they came to a major crossroad. He rode slowly forward and looked up and down the street before waving them on.

They soon approached the main bridge in the centre of the city. It was still standing and only slightly damaged by fire and weaponry. Bodies had been pushed out of the way to clear a path down the main road. Bruce looked up at the tall buildings on either side of them, walls disfigured by fire and arrows still embedded. He saw the tip of an arrow poke out from a window.

"Ambush!" he screamed.

Five goblins emerged from under the bridge. More appeared in the buildings. They were hideous creatures. Scars covered their skin. They all had sharp, twisted daggers in their wretched hands. Some had random bits of armour on and they all wore loincloths.

Theodore heard the shout and urged his horse into a gallop heading towards the bridge, sword and spear at the ready. Helena and Bruce pulled their horses to either side of his. Arrows rained down around them as the rest of the horses joined in the gallop. The archers in the group began shooting arrows back at the buildings. With squeals, some goblins fell from the windows, arrows protruding from their bodies.

The front horses approached the goblins waiting on the bridge, wicked grins spreading across their faces. Theodore raised his spear and thrust it into the middle goblin. Helena ran down the one in front of her and sliced off the head of the goblin to the side, in one move. Bruce was riding towards the goblins when an arrow from above landed into the leg of his horse. Animal and rider tumbled to the ground.

Bruce sprang up, dodging a wild swing from one goblin and blocking a second thrust from another. He kicked the first goblin as it tried to right itself and forced it backwards over the edge of the bridge, sending it crashing into the river below. The second goblin made another swing at him. Bruce blocked with one sword and stabbed the goblin through the chest with the other. As it collapsed, he looked around.

There were more goblins streaming out of side streets all along the road behind them. One rider from Cosando, Harold also had his horse brought down but there were too many goblins around him. As Bruce watched, Harold got a sword through the chest. Most of the others were safely over the bridge by now. The last warrior from Cosando, reached out a hand as he rode past and swung Bruce up behind him. Together they galloped across the bridge after the others.

The group kept riding hard until they were well out of the city, leaving the goblins far behind and killing those that appeared from buildings close to them. They slowed down but did not stop for a while. On a command from Theodore, they left the road and entered the forest that flanked the road on both sides. Only when they found a clearing far enough from the road did they stop to set up camp. One of the riders from the Empire, called Zack, had an arrow in the stomach and died from his wound soon after.

"Gods, we were lucky any of us got out of there alive," said Bruce when they sat down by the fire.

"We lost two warriors and two horses to those goblins," said Theodore.

"And the element of surprise," said Helena. "They'll tell their boss and the whole plan will go wrong."

"They won't tell," said Theodore.

"How do you know?" she asked, surprised.

"Because those didn't look like soldiers to me; they were just scavengers. None of the officer goblins appeared. If they do tell anyone, they'll probably be killed for letting us escape. We still have the benefit of surprise. Now, we need to rest. We are deep in enemy territory. We must be very careful and spend nights in cover. These creatures reportedly have good night vision. We'll spend tomorrow preparing and recovering and set out the next morning."

He got up from the fire and went into his tent. The rest of the troops followed, until only Bruce and Helena remained by the fire, with two other soldiers around the perimeter on watch.

"He's a good fighter," said Bruce after a while.

"Aye and he's a good leader. We're lucky he knows the area so well," said Helena then looked at Bruce as he winced when moving over. "You didn't get hurt, did you, when you fell?"

"No, just a little bruised."

"So sad, Harold, though."

"He was unlucky. Could've been any of us. At least he died fighting. He killed a good few of them before they got him."

"There will be more before this is over. Might as well enjoy this night and day while we have them," she said and headed to their tent with Bruce following soon after.

3: The Legacy

They buried Zack the next day. Then treated their own wounds and looked at maps to plan for the next stage of the journey. The morning after that they set out to continue their mission.

As they rode cautiously down the road, Bruce heard the low growl of an animal. Trees were encroaching on the road on either side. Bruce looked around but saw nothing suspicious. After a second or two, he watched a shadow detach itself from the trees. It began walking slowly, in parallel with their group. Bruce could just make out the four legs. He looked to the other side and saw more animals following them. He remembered what Theodore had said about the raiding parties. He rode forward to join Theodore and pointed them out.

"Follow my lead," whispered Theodore.

Suddenly, he spurred his horse forward and off the road. Bruce raced on behind him and after a moment of confusion, the other riders followed. The shadows came with them. Branches whipped against Bruce's face as the horses galloped through the trees. The shadows kept pace easily with the horses. As Bruce watched, one leapt out from the trees and he got a good view of what they were up against. The cougars were big creatures, almost as big as horses and camouflaged by their dark brown fur.

The cougar landed on the rider beside Bruce and he crashed to the ground, with the big cat on top of him. The horse he had been riding veered off to the side where another cougar took it down.

Theo's horse broke through the trees and entered a large clearing; when he reached the centre, he dismounted quickly. The other riders poured in behind him and followed his lead. They all unsheathed their weapons. The cougars entered the clearing behind them and fanned out. They had the soldiers completely surrounded.

A cougar leapt forward towards Bruce. It fell short, a low whine escaping its lips, a crossbow bolt sticking out of its side. More bolts came flying out of the trees, landing among the circling cougars. The surviving cougars disappeared back among the trees, knowing they couldn't kill the unseen archers.

Bruce looked around at his soldiers and then back towards the trees. All the cougars had fled the clearing. Suddenly, a woman dropped out of a tree. She wore light armour and carried a spear in one hand and a crossbow on her back. Her skin was as dark as Theodore's. She looked at the riders.

"Don't move," she commanded. "Crossbows are on you. Now, who are you? I'd answer quickly if I was you."

***

Alexander and General Tyson arrived back at Cosando City. They had spent the week, after inspecting the Pass of Titus, visiting the two other fortresses in the duchy. Training programs had been increased at both of them. Defences had been improved, though if a real battle occurred all troops would go to the city and present one united front. All hoped that Bruce would accomplish his mission, making the preparations unnecessary.

When Alex and Tyson reached the throne room, they found the Duke and Lord Marcus already deep in conversation.

"Ah, General Tyson, what have you to report?" asked the Duke.

"We have visited both forts and the Pass, Your Grace. They have increased all defences and more troops are being trained up. I would advise you to send another garrison to the Pass. If there is an attack it will be there, sir. I would also advise you to set up a watch post further out. Maybe we could rebuild the Empire's outpost on the other side and use it for our own. We need a way of receiving advanced warning of an attack or a gathering army so that we send more troops to the Pass, sir. We certainly need more troops at the outpost to withstand any goblin raids."

"Thank you, General. Marcus will see to it that those recommendations are carried out. Meanwhile, I have received word from the other dukes that they are also taking precautions and stepping up their armies." The Duke turned to Alex. "Alexander, I have a task for you. Even with the armies from the other dukes, I'm not sure we will have enough troops. Marcus suggested it and I think it is a good idea; I want you to travel to the Islands of Hostiban."

"But, father, the other dukes won't like that. We have fought them for so long, they won't trust them."

"I know, I know. But we have had a truce for five years now and we need all the help we can get. This war will affect them too. I have already sent a letter to Duke Richard of Sirona. He will see to it that a ship is there waiting to take you to the islands. He may not like it but he will agree to the plan. I have heard that King Kanakore is a reasonable man. Now, you will have to take some soldiers with you. We will need someone trustworthy to lead the troops. Who do you suggest?"

"Hyperion," answered Alex, immediately.

"Hmm. What do you think of that, Tyson?"

"He is a good soldier, sir, and smart. He has served us faithfully, as has his family for many generations," said Tyson.

"Alright, it's agreed. You must leave in two weeks. A small group of soldiers should be enough. Duke Richard will supply more to sail the boat. You are dismissed. Go, and prepare."

Alex left the throne room and went in search of Hyperion.

***

"Look, we mean you no harm," said Theodore, lowering his weapon. "Some of us are from here. I was once a captain in Impoarca. We present no threat to you."

"I will decide that. Where are the rest of you from, then, if only some of you are from here?" asked the woman. Bruce could just make out more people in the trees behind her. "And why are you here?"

"The rest of us are from Cosando," said Bruce, weapon still ready. Even if Theodore was ready to trust her, he was not. "The first duchy on the other side of the Pass. And we are going to stop these creatures."

The woman looked surprised for a moment and then laughed.

"Really? I wish you good luck with that. Not that it will help. Now, I have other, more important matters to attend to," she said, turning to leave.

"Who are you?" asked Theo, stepping forward.

The woman stopped and spun on her heels back to face him.

"I thought everyone died in the goblin raids?" continued Theo. "Can you help us?"

"Of course, not everybody died! Some of us made it out. Well, we could always do with some more warriors. There are many battles to fight. Soldiers are always needed and in return, I'll tell you what I know. I'm Lilith, by the way. Welcome to The Legacy."

She led them to the entrance of an old mine, as more warriors followed in the trees and shadows. The mine had been dug into the side of a lone hill, far away from the start of the Armary Mountains. The entrance was hidden in a clump of trees and at first, the place seemed abandoned but once deep inside, they found a clean and spacious interior, well-lit by torches on the walls.

Soldiers took them into an old chamber. Bruce regarded the warriors as they entered the room behind Lilith. They wore light armour like hers, painted green and brown. They all carried spears and crossbows. Lilith took a seat at the table in the centre of the room and gestured for Bruce and Theo to do the same.

"Well, here we are," she said, once they had taken their seats.

"Who are you people?" asked Bruce.

"As I said, we are The Legacy. We are all that remains of the Empire that once had millions of inhabitants and innumerable cities. Well, we think we are the only survivors, anyway. There may be others in hiding as well. We fight against these goblins and cougars where we can."

"What is this place?" asked Theo.

"Nice, isn't it?" said Lilith, smiling. "We found it after the fall of the Capital and gathered here. It is as hidden as we can hope to get."

"How many people are left?" asked Bruce.

"Hard to say really. A couple of hundred maybe. We find more every once in a while, hiding out in destroyed villages or in the forest. Not enough to do any real damage but enough to be a nuisance. Some are here right now, some are away gathering information or fighting goblins and cougars. Now, I have some questions for you. What are you going to do to destroy the enemy?"

Bruce and Theo looked at each other.

"I don't think we should say," said Bruce. He still didn't trust her.

"Ah. A secret mission."

"All I'll say is that we have information showing a way to defeat them without fighting an open battle."

"Well, I hope it works. For all our sakes."

There was a knock at the door and another warrior strode into the room.

"Lilith, a message from Nelson. He says he has eyes on a goblin enclave at the old Castellum Fortress."

Lilith leapt from her chair.

"Finally, we have what we've waited for. If this is true, this is big. Go, gather all the warriors you can find and send them to the fortress." She turned to Bruce and Theo as the warrior hurried from the room. "We could use your help with this. Afterwards, in return, I'll tell you all I know of the road from here. I don't know much but it could be of benefit to you."

Bruce and Theo looked at each other again and then nodded at Lilith.

"We'll help," said Theo.

"Good. Follow me." She left the room.

Bruce gathered up his own warriors and followed her. They brought their horses with them, even though they weren't able to ride them for most of the way as the route took them through trees rather than by the roads. Lilith raced ahead of them, with many other warriors of The Legacy speeding through the trees around them.

When they came to a halt, Bruce saw the fortress ahead of them through the trees. They tied up their horses, then Bruce, Helena and Theo went to Lilith, finding her in a rapid discussion with some other fighters. She looked up as they approached.

"Ah, there you are," she said and indicated the men around her. "This is Nelson, William and Martin, Captains in my 'army'. Lads, these are the people I told you of; the ones who will destroy the monsters."

They all smiled.

"I'd like to see that," said Nelson.

He and William looked like typical fighters, big and strong as if they had been warriors all their lives. Martin, however, appeared quite different, small and timid, more at home with his head in a book than fighting a battle.

"So, what is the plan?" asked Helena.

"Martin here is our tactician," said Lilith, turning to him.

"We have no chance of taking the fortress if they are defending it properly," he said. "We should send a small raiding party to the main gate and start fighting. Then they need to retreat as if on the run, making the goblins follow them out; they can never resist the chance of an easy victory. Meanwhile, we station more troops waiting outside to ambush the goblins. We will have our bowmen in the trees to shoot down onto them. It should be quite simple. Of course, if it does go wrong, we'll just have to resort to frantic, hand to hand fighting. Again. That's what normally ends up happening."

"Sounds good to me," said Lilith, grinning. "Any disagreements? No? Good. I'll go to the main gate. William, you lead the ambush on the ground. Nelson, you sort out the archers."

"What about us?" asked Bruce. "We want to go on the main gate."

"Do you, now?" She looked them up and down. "Alright. Just don't mess up."

The captains faded back into the trees, though for the diminutive Martin it was more of an undignified scramble to keep up with them. Bruce followed Lilith as she stealthily crept through the trees until they were in front of the fortress. More fighters appeared in the trees around them, without making a sound. Bruce looked at the main gate as he unsheathed his swords. It was wide open. A couple of goblins stood guard, although they weren't doing a very good job. They looked convinced they were all alone in the whole area. They were about to learn their mistake.

Lilith gave the signal and they left the trees at a sprint. The goblins at the gate saw them too late. Lilith's spear thrust through the first. Bruce landed on the second and sliced him through the chest. The last one had time to let off a screech before it too was killed by Theo.

Goblins poured out of buildings just inside the gate upon hearing the screech. They weren't ready though. The warriors killed the first dozen that came out before the ones behind even knew a fight was on. Once they realised, however, they came out fighting. Bruce began to back up out of the gate, as did the fighters around.

The goblins flowed out after them. Then, the ambush began. Arrows rained down from above on top of the goblins. Legacy fighters left the trees and began attacking the goblins on all sides. The goblins thrashed around in confusion; some even killed their own comrades. And then it all went wrong for the attackers.

Bruce heard horns sounding behind him and looked back. A huge goblin raiding party raced towards the fort, mounted on cougars. They had spotted the battle and rushed to join in. The ambushers became the ambushed. Legacy fighters found themselves surrounded and some got cut off from the main group. Archers in the trees tried to help but had to be careful not to hit their own warriors.

Bruce heard a goblin screaming a warning and looked over to see smoke rising above the fortress. One of the goblins in the fighting had knocked over a brazier and now the fortress was ablaze. As Bruce watched, the arch over the gate crashed down, crushing many goblins. More Legacy fighters came out of the trees, abandoning their bows. They were quickly killing all of the goblin raiding party. The goblins from the fortress found themselves caught between a renewed attack and a burning fortress. They were quickly dealt with.

A cheer went up from the Legacy fighters as the last of the goblins perished. Bruce sheathed his swords and hugged Helena who had arrived next to him. All the warriors were withdrawing from the blazing fortress. Bruce and Helena found Theo and together they went over to Lilith.

"Hey! You survived!" she said. "It was tough going there for a while but we made it."

"Did you lose a lot of troops?" asked Theo.

"Not too many. Only about twenty. And you?"

"We lost three of ours. Now, listen. You said you could tell us about the road ahead?"

"A little. I don't know too much myself, except that the main road over the mountain is still there but heavily guarded. If I was you, I'd take the other road. It is less developed and longer but there will be fewer goblins on it. To reach it, turn off at Temple Junction. Do you know it?" Theo nodded. "Good. You'll know it anyway. Also, you won't encounter a lot of the cougars there anymore. Almost all of them have moved down here. What you'll find on the other side, I don't know. Good luck to you. I hope you succeed."

She shook each one by the hand.

"Good luck, Lilith. I hope you can keep the Legacy going," said Theo as they left her.

4: The Dragon

The day after leaving the Legacy they reached the foothills of the Armary Mountains and passed a large temple, now in ruins. Just ahead lay a junction. They took Lilith's advice and turned off the main road then travelled cautiously by day and camped under cover at night. They only built a fire when necessary.

"Theo," asked Bruce one night. "Do you have a family to go back to after this?"

They were both on watch in a wide clearing surrounded by trees. Bruce and Theo had grown to be friends during the long days and nights they had spent together.

"I hope so."

"Hope?"

"I have a wife and two children," replied Theo. "When this all started, I was stationed in a fort near the village I had grown up in. My family had lived in the village for generations. My wife came from there as well. The village got raided. My squad of troops managed to get there pretty quickly and chased the goblins and wolves away. My family had been lucky enough for our home not to be attacked. My brother and his family did not fare so well. They were already dead by the time I got there. After that, I sent my wife and children to one of the islands off the coast. I just hope they made it and are safe."

They sat in silence for a while.

"Most of the warriors lost family to this war," said Theo. "Many of the homes were destroyed, wives, children, brothers, sisters, parents slaughtered. Felltear, for example, lost his whole village quite early on. His garrison was supposed to be guarding that region but the commander had called them away to protect a fortress. When they got back a couple of days later, all the villages had been burned down, all the people slaughtered. Felltear was a different man after that. He still blames his commander for that mistake."

"This shows why they must be stopped," said Bruce. "I mean, they slaughter women and children needlessly, almost as if it is a sport."

"I agree. That's why I am on this mission, to protect those people that still live. I pray that I get another chance to see my family. We have to destroy this crystal ball," said Theo, then looked around. "Enough talk. Our turn is over. Let's get some rest."

The next day, as the riders began climbing the mountains, they noticed the trees grew sparser. It also felt colder. The paved road turned into a rocky path as it wound up the side of the mountain range and across it. Once on the mountain, Bruce began seeing more signs of goblins. They passed the odd bone or pile of ashes. They were much more cautious as the threat increased. Six people stayed on watch each night, two per shift. They camped at night wherever they could find a suitable place, normally in random clearings with a couple of trees around the edge.

Bruce woke up first one morning, as he often did. They were a couple of days up the mountain. He looked around to see who was on watch. He saw Aran sitting against a tree and went over to check up on him.

"Hey, Aran, anything unusual last-" Bruce stopped when he saw Aran's face. He was pale and staring into nothing. And then Bruce saw the blood. His clothes were soaked in it. He lifted his head and saw the slash through the neck.

"Dear Gods," he muttered. "Theo! Get over here!"

As the camp came to life, Theo walked over to Bruce.

"What is-" he saw Aran. "Oh no."

He knelt down to examine the body. All the soldiers came to see what had happened. Helena paced carefully around the outside of the camp, looking at the ground.

"Who was on watch with him last night?" asked Bruce.

"Lieutenant Felltear, I think," said one of the warriors.

"And where is he?"

All the soldiers looked around, suddenly noticing his absence. None of them had a clue.

"Damn! Alright, everyone, begin taking down camp and look on the ground for any signs. Helena, Theo, come over here."

"The cut looks from a goblin blade," said Theo.

"There are goblin tracks leading away as well. I couldn't make out if there were any human tracks with them," said Helena.

"How could they have got so close without him raising the alarm? And where is Felltear?" asked Bruce. "This doesn't make any sense. I mean, why kill one guard and capture the other, then leave the rest of us here alive?"

"I don't know," said Theo. "We'll just have to be more careful. Three guards each shift from now on. Now, let's get out of here."

After continuing the journey, Bruce walked past the cooling remains of fires. His hand closed around the hilt of one of his swords. His other hand gripped the horse's rein behind him. The path had opened out into a large flat area. On one side, a mountain peak rose high above them. On the other, a deep, dark chasm cut a gap in between mountains.

Bruce knelt by one of the fires. The embers were still hot. Someone was close. Or something. He signalled for the group to stop. They needed to rest for a while and here seemed as good a place as any. Bruce needed to think about what these remains meant. He needed to know what lay up ahead, waiting for them. He turned to look around the clearing and saw a hand sticking out of the chasm. He drew his swords as a hideous body followed the hand. The goblin was holding a notched dagger in his hand. More followed him, pulling themselves out of the chasm. Each held a dagger or sword in their hand and all of them had crooked grins on their faces.

Bruce's warriors bunched together, weapons at the ready. They were outnumbered two to one at least. The first goblin stepped closer towards them. He seemed to be the leader of this gang. He grinned back at his companions, before looking at the riders.

"Lookee what we have here," he squealed.

Bruce hated the voice immediately. It was wretched. A high-pitched whine, speaking in an unnatural tongue. "The Master will be sooo pleased that we have you. We will have sooo much funnn together." The goblin began cackling.

"Step forward if you're so confident!" roared Bruce, unable to bear the sound of the voice, dragging out the words a second longer.

"Why don't you just drop your weapons and come with usss?" hissed the goblin, grinning. "We won't hurt youuu."

"You'll have to kill us before we go anywhere."

"If that's your wishhhhh."

The goblin took another step forward before he was burnt to ashes.

A spurt of flame had shot out of the chasm behind them, incinerating all the goblins. Bruce stared in shock, his mouth hanging open. Huge talons appeared gripping the side of the chasm, followed by a giant, blood red head. It launched itself into the sky, massive scarlet wings unfolding and beating to propel the beast higher and to fly around the peak above them.

"DRAGON!" screamed the soldiers.

***

Alexander knocked on the door to his father's room and entered after hearing his father shout a response. A week had passed since the decision to go to the Islands. He found his father sitting at a small table over by a window, indicating for Alex to take the seat opposite.

"Let's talk. And play," said the Duke, pointing to the game board in front of him.

'Drakanimo' was an old game and very complicated. The Duke always enjoyed playing it and so did Alex. It demanded both strategy and skill; perfect for Alex.

They gathered their starting hunters and wolves in silence. Alex chose the black pieces. He always did. The black dragon looked cooler in his eyes as a child and was said to be the most powerful. Of course, that didn't matter in the game but Alex still picked the black. Once the pieces were arranged in their caves, dens and towns, Alex began.

"How goes the preparation?" asked the Duke after a while, making a *clink* as he moved a pack of wolves across the board.

"Pretty well, father. I am getting more training in and Hyperion is picking the troops with care." *Clink* as Alex's hunting party moved in front of the pack.

"Good, good," said his father.

The game progressed silently, apart from the *clinks* as pieces moved back and forth across the board, waging war.

"Interesting game, this," his father said. Alex nodded. *Clink*. "Not many skilled players anymore. Who can find the time to enjoy a game?" *Clink*. "Bruce never played much. Maybe if he comes back, he will learn."

Alex noted the 'if' instead of 'when'. *Clink*.

"Very intriguing game," his father continued a couple of minutes later. *Clink*. "Did you know, Father Zeno says there is a similar game described in the six texts?" *Clink*. "He says it is played by the Gods. Seems far-fetched to me, but maybe." *Clink*. "This game always reminds me of the way life is." He gave a little chuckle. "Mind you, I haven't seen any dragons." *Clink*.

Alex watched as his father became more and more engrossed in his own thoughts, forgetting Alex.

"But the dragon controls the wolves and hunters," said the duke. "Makes them fight for it. It sits nice and safe in its cave unless the rest of the pieces fail." *Clink*. "We all have our dragons, forcing us forward. And there is nothing we can do but keep going and hope we live long enough to matter." *Clink*.

The duke shook his head and looked up, remembering Alex was there.

Clink. "Go, Alex. I have kept you too long. I'm sure you don't want to listen to the ramblings of an old man. We will finish the game another time." *Clink* as the Duke moved his wolf pack. "It will give you time to think of how to beat me."

Alex stood up and left the room, leaving his father sitting in his chair, staring out of the window, watching the city.

***

Bruce scrambled behind some rocks off to the side of the path, soldiers beside him doing the same. The dragon swooped down, fire leaping out of its mouth in great jets, killing the soldiers and horses that didn't move fast enough. It continued its flight, rising high up above them, its roar shaking the very mountain.

Bruce gave a shout for bows and crossbows to be readied. The surviving warriors pulled out the weapons from wherever they could find them and aimed upwards. They watched as the beast finished its rise and turned around towards them. Through the layers of his fear, Bruce realised what a magnificent creature it was.

The dragon began falling back towards the ground. Bruce readied the crossbow he had brought with him from the Legacy. The dragon was approaching. It opened its great jaws. Bruce could see the flame building up.

All the soldiers fired their arrows. Most clattered against the tough scales, though a few cut holes through the wings. The dragon let out a screech of rage and pain. Bruce watched as it scooped up a warrior in its talons. It climbed high into the sky again, its wings beating hard. The dragon reached the pinnacle of its flight and hovered in the air. It released the soldier gripped in its talons. Bruce could hear the man screaming before he crashed into the rocks far below the hovering beast.

Arrows were loaded as the dragon began another dive. Bruce got another bolt into his crossbow. They had to finish this soon before the whole group was killed. The dragon approached once more, flame already spewing forth from its mouth. Again, the soldiers let their arrows fly, hitting the dragon. Bruce knew they weren't enough. He rolled out from behind his cover and looked up at the approaching beast as it took a deep breath, preparing for another burst of flame.

Bruce took aim. He watched as the dragon prepared to release its pent-up fury. He fired. The bolt flew forward and sunk deep into the creature's eye. The dragon let out a great roar of pain. Its wings flapped wildly, trying to keep the huge body in the air. It began to rise again but not fast enough. Its legs clipped the ground and the wings faltered. The whole underside hit the ground, skidding forward at a terrifying speed. Bruce watched as the dragon crashed headfirst into the side of the mountain, its wings folded beneath it and finally, it lay still.

5: The Dead

Bruce walked cautiously towards the body of the dragon; the rest of the uninjured group crept behind him. The body just lay there, immobile, its red scales flattened and still. Bruce crept around it to look at the dragon's head. No breath. The face and nose were smashed in from the crash into the mountain. The dragon had been moving at such speed that it had actually rebounded back a small way from the rock wall.

"Thank Thaddeus, it's dead," he said, more to himself than anyone else.

One of the soldiers beside him stepped over an outlying paw and next to the dragon's face. Bruce almost shouted out, not too sure of his own assessment. But the warrior knew what he was doing.

After a moment the soldier glanced over and saw Bruce looking at him.

"You're right, sir. He is quite dead, obviously," he said. "We were lucky, sir. It could have been a lot worse."

"What do you mean, Dordon?"

"He is quite young, sir, for a dragon. Probably no more than fifty years old."

"How do you know?"

Dordon stepped back towards the head and indicated for Bruce to follow.

"See the horns here, sir?" The warrior indicated two horns growing on top of the dragon's head, with a number of smaller ones forming a line between them. "These horns are very small.

If he had grown to his full size, they would have been massive, bigger than an arm. The whole dragon is quite small compared to what I have heard them described as. Also, he didn't try to control us. It is written that full-grown dragons have the ability of Drakanimo and can control minds. He couldn't."

"How do you know it is a 'he'?" asked Bruce.

"Males generally have more horns around their head and necks, meant to impress the females."

Bruce nodded, before turning and heading back to the rest of the group. The riders were getting ready, preparing their horses. Bruce found his own and made sure it had everything he needed packed in the saddlebags. They had lost six of the warriors and more had been injured. But Bruce knew they couldn't stop yet. It still was barely past midday. They had to keep moving.

The night after the dragon attack, Bruce sat down on the log beside Dordon. They were on watch in the middle of a small clearing, at the side of the path.

"So, Dordon, how do you know so much about dragons?"

"My father was very interested in dragons, sir. He says he saw one, once, flying high over the mountains. I don't know if it's true but he brought me a lot of books on dragon lore and I learned what I could."

"I didn't know dragons still existed," admitted Bruce. "I thought they were all dead if they were ever alive at all. I definitely didn't think we would ever see one on our journey."

"I know, sir. Most of them have been wiped out, killed off fighting humans and each other. They never attacked the duchies much, anyway. They like to live in the mountains and the mountains near us are too small."

"Tell me about dragons. I have never read much about them and it will be good to talk about something to pass the time."

"Well, their true name is Drakaks, though they are called dragons most of the time," Dordon began. He looked glad to be able to show someone all that he knew. "There are three types of dragons. The first are the Fire Drakaks. They are like the one we killed today. They are red and can breathe fire. They are nearly wiped out, as they lived around these mountains. Then, there are the Ice Drakaks. They are fully white and can freeze animals with their breath. They live to the far north of the continent, where it is rumoured that the whole land and mountains are covered in ice. They don't meet humans often, as it is too cold for us.

"Then, there is the final type. They are the rarest and the most powerful: the High Drakaks. They are completely black. They can breathe flames as hot as lava and can also freeze anything. They are bigger and stronger than the other dragons. There have been no sightings of any of them for centuries and it is hoped that they are all killed off or moved away.

"Dragons are very smart, said to be smarter than humans. They can do Drakanimo, the ability to control creatures and humans. The board game is based on that. Most dragons avoid actually fighting themselves, preferring controlling other creatures to do that. They love gold and collect vast mounds of it in their caves. They can live in groups, called Storms and work together to gather gold and kill other Storms."

"Will we see anymore, do you think?" Bruce hoped not. By the sound of it, next time none of them would survive.

"I doubt it. It is rare to even see one. This was just a young one, lost from its family. With the goblins here and all, they may have moved deeper into the mountains. No point drawing unneeded attention to themselves. And they definitely won't work with the goblins' Master. They don't like having someone other than a dragon in charge of them. They would die rather than submit."

Bruce nodded. He watched as Dordon stood up and began walking the perimeter. He thought back over what he had just learned and hoped there were no more ahead.

***

Alexander handed another book over to Hyperion. They were in the massive library at the back of the palace. Shelves lined all the walls, thousands of books filling up all available space. Windows high in the walls let in a small amount of light. Lamps were located all around the room, covered when not in use.

Alex and Hyperion had spent a couple of days going through everything in the library, trying to find any books on the Islands of Hostiban. There weren't many. In the war room, they discovered some maps but these didn't offer much help. The duchies had fought with the people of the Islands for centuries. They had never taken the time to learn about them or their land.

The Duke strode into the room, followed by Lord Marcus and another man behind him.

"Ah, Alexander, Hyperion, I thought I would find you here," said the Duke. He looked at the books in front of them. "Find anything useful?"

"Not much, father."

"Sadly, we have never taken much notice of what they did before. Anyway, I want you to meet Thomas." He pointed to the man behind Marcus. "He will be going on the trip as well. He is a scholar and knows the most about the Islands of Hostiban."

Alex turned to look at the man. He was smaller and older than Alex. He had a big, black beard but was completely bald other than that. He nodded to them.

"My Lord Duke, are you sure that's a good idea?" asked Marcus, looking worried.

"Yes, yes, Marcus, I'm sure. He'll be helpful. Well, I better be going. Good luck with your preparations. You have three days until you set off."

He turned and left, with Marcus trailing after him.

***

Bruce led the remaining eleven soldiers along a narrow ledge. A couple of days had passed since the dragon attack. They were riding less and less now as the path became more treacherous. Clearings were rarer so they set up camp whenever they could, even if there was an hour or two left of the light.

Bruce looked up the mountain when he heard some rocks tumble. He stopped walking for a moment as he listened out. He started to edge forward again, bringing his horse on behind. He heard a loud crash and looked around to see boulders tumbling down the slopes above and some goblins lumbering away, not using any path.

"Move!!" Bruce shouted and began running forward, dragging his horse behind him.

The other warriors were slower to react but once they saw the boulders, they sped up. Some weren't fast enough.

Bruce reached the end of the ledge and into a wide clearing and looked back. More soldiers came off with him but the boulders were right above them. Theodore leapt forward into the clearing just as the bigger boulders hit. Not all the soldiers were as lucky. The path had been damaged and some of them crashed over the edge with the boulders.

"Damn!" Theo cursed. "How many did we lose?"

"Two riders and three horses," said Bruce, after he had counted.

"How the hell did that happen?" asked Helena.

"The goblins. They pushed some boulders to start the rockslide," said Bruce. "It's getting dark. We'll have to stay here for the night. We'll move on in the morning."

"Be ready," said Theo. "There are many goblins on this mountain."

They passed an uneasy night. None of the soldiers were able to get much sleep. Those on guard had their bows at hand the whole time in case any goblin decided to attack. When dawn finally broke, they packed up quickly and made ready to continue on the track.

Bruce was about to leave when a goblin appeared from above. He landed in front of Bruce, at the edge of the clearing. He was what Theo had called an officer goblin. He held a large spear in his hand with a metal spike on each end. He towered over Bruce, and had a large helmet on his head. Bruce looked into his face to see a hideous mouth snarl down at him. Two vicious tusks jutted out from inside the bottom lip. Bruce glanced around to see more goblins appearing at different places in the clearing. Bruce's warriors drew their weapons and gathered into a circle, waiting.

Suddenly, some humans appeared behind the officer. Bruce was thrown off balance as he thought he recognised some of them. But it wasn't possible that they could be here, could it?

"Harold? Aran? Zack?" he asked. "How are you here? We saw you die. Didn't we?"

The one who looked like Aran smiled a crooked grin. He leapt forward and stabbed the man next to Bruce. Bruce swung at Aran's head before he could recover and it flew off. The body hit the floor and crumbled to dust.

"They're not real!" Bruce shouted. "They're dead people!"

The officer goblin made a signal with his hand and suddenly all the goblins and the dead leapt forward and attacked Bruce's group. The officer made a clumsy swing at Bruce but he ducked swiftly under it and thrust one of his swords into the officer's skin but not deep enough. The officer grabbed Bruce and swung him around into the back wall of the clearing. He readied his spear to thrust it into Bruce when Helena landed on his back, sticking her daggers into him.

Theo, meanwhile, was fighting both Harold and Zack. They had already slain two warriors who hadn't been expecting to fight old friends. Theo ducked a swing from Zack and kicked him back. He blocked Harold's sword with his shield and thrust his own sword deep into his chest. Theo turned to face Zack as Harold crumbled to dust behind him. Zack jumped up and brought his sword down with force onto Theo's raised shield. Theo swung the hilt of his sword into Zack's face and stuck the blade deep into him, watching him crumble to dust.

Theo swung around to face his next enemy, sword raised. As he looked around, an arrow pierced his leg and he stumbled and fell.

"You?" he asked as he saw his attacker walking towards him. "You're not even dead."

"I know." His attacker grinned.

"Why are you doing this then?"

"Does it matter anymore?"

His attacker reached him and picked up Theo's fallen sword. He looked at it for a second as Theo tried to stand up. The attacker returned his gaze to his target and thrust it deep into Theo's chest. The killer looked around to make sure no one was watching before hurrying away.

The officer goblin finally managed to shake Helena off his back but by then he was in pain. Bruce was back on his feet and kept slashing at the officer, forcing him back. Most of his thrusts were blocked but enough landed to annoy the officer. The officer let out a deep bellow of rage. He raised his spear over his head and readied to make a final attack at Bruce. Bruce ducked to the side before the officer could make the swing. The officer experienced a moment of confusion before he noticed Helena running towards him. He realised what she was planning and tried to move out of the way but was not fast enough. Helena jumped and planted both feet on the officer's chest, pushing him backwards and over the edge of the clearing, down the side of the mountain.

Bruce pulled Helena to her feet and looked around the clearing. The goblins were fleeing after seeing their commander go over the side but that brought little joy to the warriors. Only two soldiers were still on their feet, the others dead or fatally wounded. Only four horses were left, the rest slain by accident or fleeing off the edge in their panic. Suddenly, Bruce saw Theodore leaning against a rock.

"Oh, no," Bruce muttered as he ran over to him.

Theo opened his eyes when he heard Bruce coming and gave him a small smile. Something flashed in Theo's eyes as he remembered. He grabbed Bruce's hand and pulled him towards him.

"Be… careful…" he wheezed out. "There… is… a… tr-," he coughed out blood and tried again. "He's… alive… Traito-"

He died before he could finish his sentence.

"Lord Osias awaits, my friend," said Bruce, loosening the grip on his hand.

6: The Cave

Bruce and the remaining two warriors gathered the fallen together and built a mound over them. Helena checked to see if there was anything that could be done for some of the others. After an hour, the last of the wounded died. He was buried along with the others.

"We're going to split up," Bruce said after they had finished burying the dead. "Darius, James, you two will go back to Cosando. You are to take word of what has happened and warn them about these dead people." He kicked one of the piles of dust near him. "You can take all four horses; we will have no more need for them. Try to take as little rest as possible. Switch horses often to give the others a break. Helena and I will continue the mission. Do you understand all that?"

"Yes, sir!" they chorused and saluted.

"Good luck to you. Be careful." Bruce saluted back and watched them take the horses and set off back across the damaged ledge.

"We're going to have to be extra careful now," said Helena once the others were out of sight. "There will be more goblins the closer we get."

"And if these ones bring word to their master of our group, plenty more will set out to get us," said Bruce, turning to face the way forward. "Might as well get going now, then."

Three days' on, Bruce ducked an arrow and pulled Helena around the corner as another sailed past. They had been fending off goblins almost non-stop with no time to rest. The goblins feared them too much to get close, so instead, they fired arrows at them from above. Any that did get close were swiftly stabbed or thrown over the side. They had seen no more officer goblins. Until now.

Bruce waited for a goblin to come around the corner and then tossed him over the side. Helena shot the next two goblins that were going after their friend too fast to stop. Bruce knew that would slow down the ones behind for a couple of seconds until the officer goblin caught up. He could see a cave up ahead off to the side but knew entering there would be very dangerous. There would only be one entrance and one exit.

Helena had just gone past the entrance of the cave when another officer goblin appeared in front of her. Bruce glanced behind to see the first had caught up, blocking the path back. More goblins were appearing behind both officers, snarling at their trapped prey. Bruce grabbed Helena and pulled her into the cave after him.

Once inside, the cave opened out into a small room. It was dark in there and cold. Bruce and Helena turned around once they reached the far wall, swords at the ready. They weren't going to give in without a fight. The two officer goblins were in the centre, a couple of steps in from the entrance. They walked forward slowly, wicked grins on their faces. They were going to enjoy this.

As Bruce and Helena watched, a shadow detached itself from a ledge above the goblins. It landed gracefully in front of the officers who stepped back in surprise. Bruce saw the light glint on a blade in the figure's hand and suddenly it leapt forward at the officer goblins. It was the most elegant attack Bruce had ever seen. The figure leapt from goblin to goblin, dodging their clumsy swipes and slashing each figure as it passed.

In a couple of seconds, it was over. The figure straightened up as the last goblin keeled over behind it. All the goblins, including the officers, were dead. And this figure had done it with no apparent effort. Bruce raised his blades in case they were next. The figure smiled.

"My cave," it said. "Their grave."

***

Alexander watched from the balcony of his room as more and more people arrived each day, abandoning the small farms and villages their families had lived in for generations. Every town across the duchy experienced the same; crowds of people seeking refuge in the highly populated areas. They all knew that more soldiers patrolled the cities and towns than in the countryside. Most of the young men arriving and some of the women too signed up for the army almost immediately. Alex didn't know where they could house this influx of people but his father would have to deal with it. At least until Bruce had succeeded and the threat was vanquished.

Alex turned and went inside. He was leaving soon but first, he had to attend a meeting in the throne room, to discuss the final preparations for his journey to the Islands of Hostiban. When he arrived, he found General Tyson and Lord Marcus already in consultation with his father. Hyperion entered moments later followed by Thomas, the scholar.

"Ah, Alex, it's good you are here," the Duke said. "You should hear this news too before you leave. Tyson, you were saying something new had occurred?"

"Yes, Your Grace. Just received a message," said Tyson. "It arrived by bird from Gultrum Outpost, our new position beyond the Pass."

"And what did it say?"

"The captain there, Captain Howard, says the outpost is fully operational. They have encountered no goblins as of yet but signs are all over there, sir. However, he has reported sightings of these mountain cats, or cougars, describing them as very large but also stealthy. They do not roar like other big cats but their growls strike terror in all who hear them. They have lost two horses to these animals already. Also, the goblins use hollowed-out animal horns to communicate with each other; these can be heard in the distance.

"The outpost is located just off the side of the main road, within a clearing in the forest that stretches most of the way from the Pass to Impoarca. From the goblin horns and other means, they can recognise when a big group is gathering. Unfortunately, the surrounding forest will allow a small group of goblins to sneak past. But at least it will alert us of any major group approaching."

"Does he ask for anything?" said the Duke.

"No, sir."

"Good. That's good. What about the other forts?"

"They are still receiving more recruits. Nothing new to report there, sir."

"Marcus, what are we doing about all the people arriving in the city?" the Duke asked, turning towards his advisor.

"Sir, we are finding any accommodation we can to give to them. The others are pitching tents behind the city, with extra defences being built around them. It is all we can do at the moment, sir."

"Well, keep me updated." He turned towards Alex. "Are you ready for your journey?"

"Yes, father."

"Good. Marcus has sent a message to King Kanakore, informing him of your visit. A message has also been sent to Duke Richard. A ship, fully-manned will be waiting there for you, as well as extra guards who know the islands well. Are your own guards prepared?"

Hyperion stepped forward.

"Yes, Your Grace. A select group of soldiers have been picked, sir. They are all loyal and excellent warriors."

"Good. Go, then. Bring back some troops and let's hope, with some better news."

Alex left the throne room and headed for the stables where his soldiers awaited him.

***

As the figure approached Bruce and Helena. Bruce raised his swords, anticipating an attack. It never came. The figure strode past them and pressed his hand against the wall. A section of it swung back to reveal a well-lit stone cavern beyond. The figure beckoned for them to follow and went ahead without waiting for them to respond. Bruce glanced at Helena, who shrugged. They sheathed their blades and entered the room. They saw what he had done to the goblins and knew they stood no chance if he decided to do the same to them.

Bruce looked around as he followed. It was bigger than the cave outside and more homely. Torches hung on the walls and a fire glowed beneath a vent in the rock, through which the smoke escaped. Heads of ferocious-looking beasts hung up high on the walls and fur carpets covered the floor. In the furthest wall, they saw a strong wooden door.

Bruce couldn't hide his amazement. From the outside, you couldn't tell how big this place was nor even see the entrance when it was closed. He wondered what kind of person would decide to live in a place like this, alone in the mountain, and how they could have built it to be so comfortable.

Following this thought, he turned to examine their rescuer. Now that they were in the light, Bruce found himself facing a tall, slim man. Though after looking for a while longer, he decided man might not be the right word. His face seemed more elegant than any man's, as well as having long, pointed ears. Pure white hair flowed down to his shoulders. He looked so slender and yet Bruce had seen him take down many goblins with no apparent effort. He had laid his swords on a table in the centre of the room and Bruce wandered over to examine them.

Bruce stood gaping at them for a couple of seconds. They were of a finer quality than any other weapon he had ever seen, made by a master craftsman. They looked so sharp, Bruce felt they could cut through anything. The ends of both hilts looked broken as if they had once been one double-bladed sword. Bruce reached out a hand to touch them.

"I wouldn't do that, or you'll be lying flat," said the man, without turning.

"Who are you?" asked Bruce.

"I'm just a warrior retired, most of my days expired."

"How could you fight like that?" asked Helena.

"I was trained, and so the blood rained."

"Why did you help us? And why do you speak in rhymes? What is your name? Are you even human?" asked Bruce.

"No more of my confessions, I'll ask you the questions. Why are you two here, and not home without fear?"

"We don't have to tell you," Bruce said, after exchanging a glance with Helena.

"Outside my cave, to you help I gave. So, if you tell me, I won't kill thee."

Suddenly he appeared next to the table with the swords on it.

"We're here to defeat the goblins and their master. And you won't stop us," said Helena.

"You should go back because a good plan you lack."

"We have come this far, we won't give up now," said Helena.

The man shrugged, showing he didn't care what they did.

"You could help," she continued. "Come with us. You are the mightiest swordsman I have ever seen."

"I'm retired, no longer required."

"How about you train us, then? Just for a couple of days. Please, we need your skills if we are going to get through this land."

The man thought for a moment.

"For one week you two shall stay, then you leave and hunt your prey."

Bruce drew Helena to one side.

"Do you really think this is a good idea?" he asked.

"Yes. We need all the help we can get. We have trouble fighting two officers, never mind a whole land full of them! You saw what he did! I know we won't get that good in a week but even if we learn something, we'll be better off. Who knows what knowledge he holds."

"But-"

"Look, it will do us good to have a week without having to fight and run from goblins every day. It'll give the goblins some time to cool down and stop searching for us."

Bruce nodded wearily.

"It'll be good for us," said Helena and walked over to the man, who had observed the conversation with a knowing smile. Helena held out her hand.

"We're in," she said.

7: The Tower

Bruce and Helena endured a gruelling week of training. The rhyming man, who said his name was Primatore, worked them hard. They spent the mornings building up speed and stealth, as well as practising fighting skills. Primatore knew they didn't have the numbers to face the goblins head-on, so he decided that they must learn to sneak past, unseen by all.

They spent the afternoons learning what they could about the goblins. In the backroom behind the wooden door, Primatore had a map of this land since the goblins had taken it over. He pointed out a tower in the centre of a big city close enough to the mountains. It had once been the palace of an old kingdom before the goblins' master had claimed it. He called it Tenebris. He said that if there was a crystal ball, which he doubted, that would be where it was. He told them the master was cruel and many humans who hadn't escaped over the mountains or been killed in battles were being tortured all over the land. The dead soldiers roamed the fallen cities. Primatore said their numbers were increasing dramatically all the time.

At night, as they sat around the fire, Primatore told them stories of many wars and battles, often involving goblins. He would always be sharpening his blades against a stone as he did this. He spoke in his weird way, every sentence in rhyme. Bruce and Helena were unable to learn much of his past. He refused for a long time to tell them why he spoke in rhyme, where he was from, or even how old he was. From the way he talked about some of these battles, it sounded like he had been there himself, which Bruce thought was impossible. It wasn't until the last night he revealed his story.

"I was a Slayer for the Gods, fighting against the dark odds," he began.

"But they're not real!" Bruce cut in. He looked down as Primatore glared at him. "Sorry."

"I was the first and fought with a thirst. I followed the Lord of the Sky, and I proved a worthy ally. The very best never failed a quest. Until I was caught, my skill turned to nought. I was given a curse, could only speak in verse. I was called the Lyrical Lord, wielder of a broken sword. When I was freed, I left my creed. And so ends my story, with no hint of glory."

Primatore fell silent.

"Lord of the Sky…" muttered Helena. "Oh, my. You're an Elf?"

Primatore nodded without looking up, lost deep in his memories. The sharpening of the blade had stopped.

"How did you know that?" Bruce asked her.

"Did you ever listen to Zeno?"

"No, not really. All he talked about was how great the Gods were all the time. I soon got bored with that."

"Well, if you were really listening, you might've learned something. As kids, he would read to us from the texts. In them, they said each pair of gods had a race. For the Lord and Lady of Land, humans. For Sky, elves. For Water, merfolk. For Forests, dryads. For Underground, dwarves. And for the Afterlife, wizards. Did you learn none of that?"

"Um, some of it sounds familiar, now that you say it. And he's an elf? I thought they were just stories!"

"So did I. Until now. It makes sense though, looking at him, and the way he fought."

Primatore awoke from his thoughts.

"Time to go for rest, so we'll be at our best," he said, standing up. "Tomorrow you must be gone, likely just after dawn. You probably won't succeed but I hope you make them goblins bleed."

He turned and walked over to his bed, leaving them there to discuss their plans for tomorrow.

***

Darius glanced around at the trees on either side. It had been over two days since James had fallen, struck by an arrow as the horses sprinted through Impoarca. Yesterday, a cougar had taken a horse. The remaining three were exhausted. He was only a couple of days from the Pass. Once there, he would be safe.

As he urged his horse forward, leading the other two, a goblin horn sounded in the distance. They could be heard now and again, communicating with each other. Sometimes Darius would notice a cougar running past in the trees. He had been told that they had left the mountains but hadn't realised how many of them there were here in the woods.

Darius lived in constant fear of an arrow coming from the woods and hitting him. He had passed goblins a way back and by now the word would have gotten around. He was so tired. He hadn't slept since James died, because there would be no-one on watch. His eyes were beginning to droop shut when an arrow whizzed past his ear. Wide awake now, he sat up in the saddle and pulled out his shield just in time to block the next arrow.

Suddenly, a cougar was running beside one of the horses. It was the first clear look Darius had got; all the others being fleeting images through the trees. They were big creatures, just smaller than the horses at the shoulders but just as long and coated in dark brown fur. Darius watched as the massive shoulder muscles bunched and released as it kept pace easily with the horses.

Darius dragged his sword out of its scabbard and kicked his horse to speed it up. The cougar matched his new pace and more of the beasts appeared within the trees. With graceful agility, the original cougar leapt and brought down the horse to the right of Darius. Darius looked back to see a couple of cougars emerge from the trees to share in the meal. As he watched, a white cougar left the trees. The others backed away to let the white have the first bite, before then joining in.

Darius turned his attention back to the road in front, waiting for the next arrow. Three more came in quick succession from the trees on the left and he felt them each pound into his moving shield. He saw some goblin archers riding on the back of cougars in the trees, aiming more arrows. Darius felt a searing pain in his right arm and he dropped his shield. He looked over to see an arrow protruding from his shoulder. He bent low over his horse, avoiding another arrow by doing so. An arrow entered his leg as the hidden riders adjusted their shot. As a final arrow entered his side, Darius remembered the family he had left behind to come on this mission.

***

Alexander rode slowly through the gates of Sirona City. He led his group straight up to the palace, where servants came and took away their horses. Most of his guards stayed outside. Only he, Hyperion and Thomas went inside. They were escorted immediately to the throne room.

"His Grace, the Duke of Sirona, welcomes Lord Alexander of Cosando," announced the herald, as Alex and his group bowed.

"Alex, it is great to see you again," said Duke Richard, stepping down from his throne to shake his hand. "I trust you are well?"

"I am, thank you, sir," Alex replied. "Allow me to introduce my companions. This is Hyperion, my guard and a good friend. And this is Thomas, a scholar."

"Good to meet you," said Richard, shaking their hands. "Alex, come, walk with me."

He turned and led Alex out of a side door, leaving Hyperion and Thomas standing there. The door led out into a grand garden. Flowers bloomed to either side of the gravel path. Cherry trees, covered in blossom, stood in the nearby orchard as birds flew from their branches up into the sky. Alex looked back to see a dog relaxing on the grass while her puppies played around her.

"Beautiful, isn't it?" said Richard. "My wife loves spending time here. Sadly, she's away right now. She would have liked to see you again too."

They came to a bench overlooking the lawn and sat down together.

"And, now, to business," said Richard. "Are you sure it is a good idea to go to the Islands?"

"My father thinks so," said Alex. "You have heard about the creatures?" Richard nodded. "Well, we will need all the help we can get when fighting them. I mean, they wiped out the whole Empire in a couple of weeks!"

"I know. But these people have been our enemies for so long. We only stopped fighting them in the last five years."

"My father knows that. And he knows what he is doing."

"Yes, I'm sure he does. Your family has always excelled at these things. Well, then, I will help you in any way I can," he said, standing up. "Let's go back."

Alex followed him back into the throne room.

When they returned, Alex saw another soldier waiting with Hyperion and Thomas.

"This is Captain Lawrence," said Duke Richard, indicating the warrior. "An accomplished soldier and archer who has spent most of his life fighting the armies of the Islands. He knows them well. He will accompany you, along with other soldiers. Captain, I introduce you to Lord Alexander of Cosando."

The soldier bowed. Richard turned back to Alex.

"Your ship should be ready. Good luck."

They shook hands again before Alex left with his warriors.

***

Bruce and Helena arrived at the outskirts of the Dark City of Tenebris. They had travelled two days from the Lyrical Lord's cave, through a land crawling with goblins and dead warriors and passed many villages, some of them destroyed; the operating ones now run by goblins. The local inhabitants found themselves forced into making weapons and armour, as well as producing food for their captors and the cries of those tortured for the smallest transgression rang out as a warning to all. Throughout this land Bruce had listened to the screams of the tormented, knowing that if he failed in his mission, his own people would suffer the same fate.

They came to a clearing on top of a small hill. Most of the trees had been burnt and their ashes covered the landscape. Bruce felt his heart nearly stop as he saw how many red dragons confronted them. After the initial fright, however, he noticed their scales all torn and savaged, their blood turning the dust red. At least five red dragons had met their end there.

In the centre, lay a huge black dragon, gold lining glinting between its scales. It was twice as big as the other dragons. Many arrows and spears stuck into its flesh. It must have taken hundreds of goblins to kill it unless the Master himself had appeared. The head had been chopped off, probably taken back to some goblin city as a trophy. At least it proved Dordon's point. They wouldn't side with the goblins.

This city in front of them seemed different from the others. They could still hear the screams but they sounded muffled as if the victims languished deep in the dungeons. The goblins Bruce could see in the street looked different as well. They seemed calmer, more organised, here to do a job. Bruce sensed they had arrived at the lair of the Master.

At the centre of all activity stood the tower. It was tall, so very tall and menacing. No matter what you did in the city, no matter where you went, your gaze was drawn to the tower. It was made of smooth black stone, with few windows apart from the top floor. *That is where the ball is,* thought Bruce. *That top floor.*

Both Bruce and Helena flinched and reached for their swords as they heard a great multitude of goblins suddenly start screaming. They had been making their way stealthily along the rooftops of the buildings, heading towards the tower. They waited, frozen in fear for a moment. When no horde of goblins came running towards them, they began to relax.

"What was that scream about?" asked Bruce.

"I don't think they were screaming," said Helena. "I think they were cheering. My guess would be for a fight."

"What? As in an arena? Do you think they perform this with humans as some kind of sport?"

"From everything we know of them, it seems likely. Let's be careful."

They reached the base of the tower as the setting sun hit the horizon. They made ready to enter the tower, knowing one last push and this could be over.

***

Lilith looked up from the map on the table when a warrior stormed into the room. He was out of breath, completely red in the face.

"Lilith, we're…" he began coughing. Once he got his breath back, he continued. "Lilith, we're trapped!"

"What?"

"The goblins, they've found the entrance. They know we're here. There are so many of them! William had a group at the door. They're already dead."

"Dear Gods," Lilith muttered. "Where is Nelson?"

"He was out. On a mission. Other groups were out as well."

"Good." She turned to Martin beside her. "Is there any way to warn them not to come back here?"

"Yes, I believe so. If we go to some of the higher tunnels there will be air ducts. If we light a fire underneath them the smoke will rise out. Hopefully, they will know not to come back here. It's all we can do at such short notice. And I don't think the goblins will be willing to grant us more time to prepare."

"Alright. You take some men and do that. Remember, black smoke will be clearer." She turned back to the man who had brought the message as Martin scurried out of the room. "You, you go and get as many of our fighters as you can. Send them to the main gate. If we're gonna lose, we're gonna lose fighting. I'll go straight to the guards already at the entrance."

Lilith strode out of the room and went to get her gear. She picked up her spear and two crossbows before heading to the entrance. On her way, she passed other fighters. They fell in behind her. When she stopped at the door to the first cavern, she saw goblins busy looting the dead bodies of her warriors. They weren't prepared for an attack. With a quick glance back at her warriors she stormed through the door, firing both crossbows immediately, taking down two goblins. She tossed the bows away, knowing reloading would cost her precious time. She pulled out her spear and charged the nearest goblin. The Legacy fighters flowed into the room behind her, quickly killing all the remaining goblins. Then, as one body, they turned to face the entrance. More goblins waited there, snarling at the Legacy fighters and about to charge. Lilith gave them no chance.

"FOR THE EMPIRE!" she yelled as she rushed forward.

The shout was echoed by the warriors behind her. She crashed into the goblins, her spear already swinging. All of The Legacy remaining in the mine flowed out into the open air behind her. She slashed, she ducked, she thrust, she stabbed. Goblins fell before her onslaught. But there were too many. An arrow caught her in the stomach and still she fought on. A sword slashed a cut down the side of her face and she just turned and killed the goblin. Another arrow pierced her shoulder. She stumbled back. A swinging club smashed into her chest and she tumbled to the ground.

Just as she was about to close her eyes, she saw black smoke rising above. She smiled. The Legacy would live on. The Empire would live on.

***

Bruce and Helena entered the tower through a back door, probably the servants' entrance back before the goblins had taken control because it opened into an abandoned kitchen. No sign of any guards. Bruce thought the Master must be so full of himself that he didn't even bother to cover this entrance.

They left the kitchen and crept softly along a dimly lit corridor. They both pulled out their swords, ready for any surprises. The corridor opened into an old hall with stairs leading upwards to one side. Two goblin guards paced the hallway. Bruce and Helena used the dim light to their advantage and snuck up behind the guards, felling them silently to the floor. It seemed that their week of training with Primatore was paying off.

They began climbing the stairs. At regular intervals, they passed landings. Doors blocked their view into the rooms beyond but the ones they did glimpse looked unused and in disrepair.

Eventually, they arrived at the top and faced a door of dark oak. Bruce pushed it open cautiously, wary of any troops waiting within. When no attack came, he entered with Helena following behind. They found themselves in a massive chamber, the roof barely visible far above them. Glass windows faced out at the city on all sides. Torches lined the walls low down, making this the brightest room they had seen so far in the tower.

In the centre, on a pedestal, stood the crystal ball.

It was the most intricate piece of glassware Bruce had ever seen. It wasn't exactly a sphere. He could see that as he got closer. It had so many facets it appeared almost round and pitch black, not even the glimmer of a reflection.

"It's actually here," said Helena, staring at it. "I almost didn't believe it until now." She glanced around. "Now, be quick and destroy it. They may have found the dead goblins and be after us already."

Bruce nodded and raised a sword. He looked at the ball one last time, almost sad that he had to destroy such a fine piece of work. He shook his head, bringing himself back to the present and brought the hilt quickly onto the ball.

The crystal shattered.

Nothing happened. Bruce and Helena glanced at each other and then looked around. Suddenly, a booming laugh filled the room, seeming to come from every direction at once.

A person landed a little way from Bruce and Helena. They hadn't seen him before; he must have been hiding in some alcove high in the wall. They swung their swords but knew they would be of no use. This was no real man. He stood over ten feet tall, looming above them, clad in black armour from head to toe. The black helmet had only small slits for eyes, otherwise totally covering the face. He held a spear in one hand, similar to the ones used by officers except it was all in black and even taller than the man. And he was still laughing.

They heard the thundering of feet behind them and turned to see six officer goblins enter the room. They fanned out, forming a semi-circle around their new prisoners.

"Did you really think that would work?" asked the Master of the Goblins, as Bruce and Helena turned back to face him.

He removed the helmet from his head, placing it on the pedestal. The face underneath was freakier than any helmet. It looked almost human but too perfect. And the eyes. Eyes out of nightmares. Completely red, apart from a pinpoint of black in the centre of each. He smiled at them.

"Storm my tower, kill my guards, destroy my crystal and get away with it? Oh, that's why I love humans. Always so gullible, so naïve. Believing they can defeat anything. I mean it was so easy and so unnecessary. I could have killed your little expedition at any time. I could even have taken out your kingdoms any time I liked. But I prefer to see you struggle. To let you think that you have a chance. And you fell right into my trap, using the first plan anyone suggested. I mean, the information was mostly true but one thing you didn't know. The crystal ball only holds any importance once I have left the planet or I'm dead. So, your plan could never work. Do you want to see something? Guards, bring It forward."

Two more officers entered, escorting a man between them. Bruce and Helena knew him immediately. Lieutenant Felltear stepped forward away from the goblins, grinning. He had a couple of new cuts but other than that he hadn't changed.

"You? You're here?" asked Bruce.

"And he's not even a dead soldier," said the Master, laughing. "He was with me from the beginning. He told you about the ball in the first place. He lied, something you humans do so often and so well."

"You're alive? You traitor!" growled Bruce, advancing on Felltear.

Two officers swiftly walked up and grabbed his arms.

"More than that. He also killed Captain Theodore. And told us all about that group of rebels." The Master was enjoying himself.

"You murderer! You traitor!" Bruce broke free of his guards and managed to thrust a sword into Felltear before they grabbed him again. Felltear stumbled, clutching his chest, the grin fleeing his face.

"That's alright. He has served his purpose," said the Master, walking over to them. "But you must still be punished. There must always be punishment."

He grabbed Helena in one huge hand and held her up, facing Bruce.

"No!" Bruce tried to break out but the guards weren't letting go this time. He could see Helena's face and she looked so scared. He couldn't hear her but he could just make out her lips forming 'please' repeatedly. The Master smiled and thrust the spear through her. Bruce saw the light fade from her eyes. He fell to the floor, sobbing.

"That is just the beginning of your punishment," said the Master, leaning down towards Bruce. "You'll learn to respect me. I am Lord Diabolous, Follower of the Darkness. And you will submit. Eventually."

8: The Sea

Alexander stood on the deck of the ship and looked out at the rolling blue waves in front of him. It had been a long time since he had been to the sea. When his mother was alive, she used to take him and Bruce on trips to the coast once a year. She had been born on the island duchy of Livona and only moved to Cosando when she was in her twenties. She had always loved the sea. Seeing it again brought back memories of her to Alex. And of her final days.

She had died fifteen years ago, after a long illness. Alex still remembered her in those last days. She just lay on the bed, unable to move, or speak. It took his father a long time to recover from her death. He barely spoke for a month afterwards. Alex and Bruce hadn't been to the sea since then.

Alex came back from his thoughts as Hyperion wandered up to the rail next to him. They couldn't see the Islands. It would be a couple of days before they reached them. Natalie, Captain of the ship and a veteran of many sea battles against the Islanders, knew the course well,

"Do you think the king will listen?" asked Hyperion.

"I don't know," said Alex. "I hope so."

"Thomas doesn't know either. He said that the king might help as it will make things easier in the long run. But he said that there have been so many years of fighting that he could hold some grudges. He said these Islanders have never become friends with anyone. All they do is kill and pillage."

"Well let's hope they can change," said Alex.

Just then, a shout went up from a crew member at the rail on the other side. All of the crew and the soldiers from Sirona began rushing around. Alex and Hyperion looked at each. Alex stopped Captain Lawrence as he sped past.

"Lawrence, what is going on?" Alex asked.

"Snappy dolphins," he said brusquely before hurrying away.

"Oh, by Lykaon, not them," muttered Alex.

"Wait, what are snappy dolphins?" asked Hyperion. Alex remembered that Hyperion had rarely been to the sea before.

"They're way bigger than normal dolphins," Alex explained hurriedly. "They have massive teeth. They can jump long distances. They swim around and attack ships. They jump over the deck and catch a crew member in their mouth before landing in the water again."

"That doesn't sound good."

"It's not."

Alex saw them bring out the harpoons and went over to help. One of the crew members handed a harpoon to Alex. He had learned how to use these when they had gone fishing with his mother. He hurried over to the side of the ship and looked down.

As Alex watched, a dolphin leapt from below the surface. It was completely black, apart from the white eyes. Its mouth opened and Alex could see hundreds of razor-sharp teeth. He shot his harpoon but it barely glanced the dolphin's flipper. Its mouth closed around a crew member beside Alex before it landed in the water on the other side of the ship.

Alex quickly retrieved his harpoon before getting ready again. By this time most of the sailors and soldiers had harpoons in their hands. They were all watching the water on either side of the ship waiting for another dolphin to leap. Snappy dolphins never travelled alone.

The next dolphin leapt on the opposite side to Alex. Two harpoons hit it in the belly. The momentum still carried it over but the harpoons had ropes attached to them. The dolphin was being pulled up when another jumped. This one aimed for the ropes linking the dead dolphin to the ship. It cut right through them and the body floated to the bottom of the sea.

A final snappy dolphin leapt directly at Alex. He brought his harpoon forward and stuck straight into the dolphin's open mouth. Alex was pushed back by the force of the impact. He fell to the deck. The dolphin landed a few feet away. Immediately the crew surrounded it and thrust as many harpoons as possible to ensure its death.

Hyperion hurried over to Alex and helped him to his feet.

"You okay?" he asked.

"Yeah, I'm fine," replied Alex.

He brushed himself off as Captain Lawrence strode over to him.

"Well done, sir," he said, smiling. "Good kill. There's good eating on one of them."

"You're going to eat it?" asked Hyperion incredulously.

"Of course," Lawrence looked surprised. "Why wouldn't we? Once it's chopped up and cooked it tastes the same as any other fish. It would be a waste to throw it over the side. Now, we must resume our voyage."

Despite his grumblings, Hyperion did eat some of the dolphin and admitted it didn't taste that bad. After dinner, that night, Alex, Hyperion, Thomas and Lawrence sat around the table and discussed their plan for convincing the king of the Islands.

"So, Thomas, what should we expect when we land?" asked Alex.

"Well, it is hard to say with these people," replied Thomas. "They seem to do everything randomly. The only thing they consistently stick to is fighting."

"Will they help us?"

"Well, they will hear us out and decide if it's in their best interest to help us."

"Of course, it's in their best interest!" exclaimed Hyperion.

"Well, they only have our word for it. And we have been at war for so long they won't know whether to believe us or not. They might think we are lying to them. They will not trust us easily."

"Will they attack us?" asked Lawrence.

"Well, not immediately anyway. But if they decide we are a threat or we are trying to trick them, then we are in trouble. In that event, we get to the boat as quickly as possible and leave. It is my opinion that we leave all the crew on the ship so that we can make a quick getaway. Only the warriors should come with us off the ship. Now, time for sleep. Who knows what tomorrow will hold. We'll reach the main island in two days."

Alex was woken up by horns sounding above him. He looked at the window in his cabin and saw the pale blue of early morning. He heard footsteps outside as he got dressed and then a loud knocking at the door.

"Come in," he said as he tied his bootlaces.

Hyperion burst into the room.

"Al, hurry!" he exclaimed. "Pirates have been spotted!"

Hyperion turned and ran back out of the room. Alex grabbed his sword and followed him to the deck. Soldiers were running around, getting their weapons and preparing. Alex strode over to Captain Lawrence. He was leaning on the rail, looking out over the water. Alex followed his gaze and could make out the black flags on two ships drawing nearer.

"Captain! Can we outdistance them?" asked Alex.

"No, sir. Their ships are faster than ours, they are blocking the direction we want to go and they have already spotted us. The only thing to do is fight."

"Is there no other way?"

"No, this is the only way. The soldiers are ready."

"Good." Alex turned and walked over to Hyperion.

"Captain says we'll have to fight, Hyp," Alex said. "You ready?"

"Yeah, I'm ready. I'll make sure our troops know. Most of them haven't fought at sea before."

"I know. We'll have to do the best we can. Make sure Thomas knows and stays inside."

Hyperion nodded and strode away. Alex turned to look at the approaching ships, close enough now for him to make out the flags. They bore the skull and crossbones of pirates everywhere but on these, the skull appeared to be on fire. Alex turned to Lawrence next to him.

"Why is the skull on fire?"

"That is the insignia of Bradok the Burner. He is the leader of the most ruthless pirate gang there is. They leave no survivors and set fire to the ships after they have looted them. They will put up a tough fight. We will have to employ some dangerous tactics. Luckily for us, they don't expect us to have soldiers aboard. The captain of this ship has beaten them a couple of times. Her crew is the best there is. Also, they want to plunder the ship, not sink it outright."

Archers from Sirona moved up and lined the rail beside Alex. He took a step back to get out of their way. His own troops were waiting behind with Hyperion. The ships moved closer. The archers set fire to the tips of their arrows and waited, careful not to touch the flames. Alex could make out the archers on the closest ship getting ready. As Lawrence shouted the order, the troops let their flaming arrows fly, raining down on the nearest boat. Some hit pirates, some missed completely. But enough landed to set the ship and sails on fire. One ship down, one to go.

Alex raised his shield just in time to block an arrow from the second ship. Others weren't so lucky. Archers made ready for a second volley but the pirates were too close to use fire. Small boats were released and sailed closer to Alex's ship. Alex ran to the rail and cut the first grappling hook as it landed. More were landing all along the rail. Alex ducked as more arrows landed among them. Suddenly the pirates jumped onboard.

Alex blocked a cutlass and slashed at the pirate in front of him. More pirates swarmed up the sides. Alex's archers stopped firing and drew their swords. The enemy archers took their chance in this break from fire, to come across themselves and then they attacked wildly. Alex blocked their swings and got in his own attacks where he could. Beside him, Hyperion fought bravely, a small battle-axe in one hand, a small round shield in the other. The pirates had superior numbers but seemed ill-prepared for the ferocity of their opponents. The soldiers of the duchies relentlessly pushed them back. One by one they fled back to the safety of their own ship. Eventually, the deck was cleared of enemy pirates. A cheer went up from the surviving crew and soldiers.

Suddenly, the shouting turned from joyful into a warning. Alex looked across to see pirate archers preparing fire arrows and within seconds they flew towards the ship. The sailors went into a frenzy of activity to put out the fires. Some Sirona archers shot back with flaming arrows of their own. Alex saw the fires on his ship swiftly extinguished but the sail was already destroyed. The pirate ship fared even less well. Before Alex's eyes, the ship slowly fell apart.

"We did well," said Lawrence, walking up to Alex. "We didn't lose too many soldiers or sailors."

"But we lost the sail," said Alex.

"Captain Natalie says there's a spare in the hull. But she is concerned about these pirates."

"Why? I thought this was a common thing that she has withstood many times before?"

"Yes, she has. But this was different. After they lose, normally they flee immediately. Otherwise, they get destroyed like we just did to them. But this crew tried to burn our ship. She says that never happens. We should be very careful about what we do from now on. Something's not right about this."

The next day they approached the main island, having passed a couple of outlying ones, the fortresses built on them a tribute to the long years of war with the duchies. Crews onboard military ships watched them sail past with interest. Duchy ships rarely went to the capital. As they entered the port, Alex took in the surroundings. On a hill in the centre of the island stood a palace. The island wasn't that big and the city seemed to cover every part of it. The hill provided the only elevation and even that was only a gentle rise. It was the most inhabitable island they had seen which explained the mass of people going about their business.

Waiting for them on the quayside, stood a squad of heavily armed soldiers.

9: The King

"Ah, I see they have the reception party ready," said Thomas, coming up beside Alexander.

"Why so many?"

"They don't trust us. Not surprising really," Thomas sighed.

Alex left him there and headed over to Captains Natalie and Lawrence.

"Are the soldiers ready?" asked Alex. "They have their own waiting."

"The troops are ready," answered Lawrence.

Alex turned to Natalie.

"You'll be here? Ready?"

"Aye, don't worry 'bout us, boss. We'll be waitin'. The crew know how to make a quick get'way."

"Good. I suppose there's nothing for it but to go."

As soon as the gangplank touched the stone quayside, Hyperion and Thomas led the way off the ship, swiftly followed by Lawrence. At an order from Hyperion, a group of armed soldiers formed a protective group around Alex. A clerk stepped forward from the waiting troops. He looked at Alex's party with disdain.

"Follow me," he said, turning on his heel and setting off down the street.

The Islanders formed themselves around Alex's group. Alex took in the surroundings as he followed the clerk. The houses looked more like huts than the buildings back home and all different with no common style. The streets seemed haphazard, unplanned and disorganized. Alex felt as if he had arrived in a bunch of villages clustered together rather than a city. And all the while the road climbed upwards, towards the palace at the centre. Out of every window and along every street, natives watched the passing group. Alex looked at the soldiers escorting them, all of them men, strong and muscular. None wore armour, in fact, they appeared bare-chested and covered in tattoos. They carried wooden spears with no metal blades and a second wooden spear strapped to their backs. Some of the more senior ones held cutlasses, similar to those used by the pirates.

Glancing around again, Alex noticed that none of the houses contained any stone; the streets consisted of gravel and most tools seemed fashioned from wood. Some of the more advanced tools were made of iron. Thinking back, the only time he remembered seeing a lot of stone occurred as they passed the fortresses on the outlying islands. It seemed they had reserved most of it for those.

They left the houses behind as they approached the palace. Stone had been used for the surrounding wall and some of the watchtowers but once through the gate, it was back to wood. A path led to the main door of the palace, via a courtyard and a garden. Guardsmen stood to attention and a few other interested observers looked on.

When they reached the main door, the clerk turned back to face the group.

"Not all of you can come inside," he said. "Only the delegate and a couple of others. They will leave their weapons behind and the rest will wait here."

Alex stepped forward and signalled for Hyperion, Thomas and Lawrence to come with him. They took out their weapons and gave them to the remaining soldiers. Once the clerk was satisfied that they were unarmed, he ordered the guards within to open up the door and he led them through down a short corridor which ended with another closed door. They passed a couple of side corridors and doorways on the way. Another guard stood waiting at this entrance and he pushed it open as they approached.

Suddenly they found themselves in a huge circular room and in the centre, facing them, appeared a massive man, tall and muscular, swathed in a red cloak and displaying dark tattoos across his bare chest. On his head rested a crown of gold and he looked down upon them from an impressive throne. Beside him sat a wizened, old man who fixed them with a piercing stare.

The clerk knelt before them, head bowed.

"My lord, King Kanakore," he said, still kneeling. "This is the group of foreigners from the duchies."

Kanakore leant forward and looked at them.

"Thank you, Scribon," he said after a moment. "You may wait outside."

The clerk got off his knees and left the room, walking backwards and still bowing. The King turned back to the visitors.

"So, you are the travellers from the duchies," he said. "It is not often we receive your kind here on friendly terms. But the times are changing." He looked at the paper in his hand. "Which of you is Lord Alexander?"

"I am, King Kanakore," said Alex, stepping forward and bowing slightly.

"It says here you have a proposition that will be in our mutual interests. What is it?"

"You have heard that the Empire has fallen?"

"Yes, I have heard that. Why should that concern me?" asked the King.

"Well, the same creatures that destroyed them will make a move for the duchies next. We will need all the soldiers we can get to defend our homes."

"That still doesn't concern me."

"If the duchies fall, it will just be you against their whole army. We believe the Pass of Titus is the best place to defend. It is narrow and can be held for a long time. We can defeat the army once and for all there, ending the threat to you and us."

"I have my islands. They will not take them. We have defended them for many years against invaders, as you well know. And now you want me to abandon them and come to the aid of the duchies?" he laughed scornfully. "I shall not do that."

"This is like no army you have faced before," said Alex. "These are not humans. They will attack again and again until you or they are destroyed. Together we can finish them. Take them on separately and we both fail!"

The King looked thoughtful. The old man next to him whispered something in his ear. He nodded.

"You have had a long journey. Rest here tonight. Tomorrow, I will give you my answer. Your men can sleep in an empty barracks. There is a spare chamber for you. Scribon!"

The clerk hurried back into the room. He knelt again.

"Show Lord Alexander to a spare chamber and his men to a barracks."

"Thank you for considering this," said Alex, bowing again before following the clerk out of the room.

King Kanakore watched the door close behind them. It had certainly been an interesting meeting. He turned to Covolar the Advisor.

"What did you think of the barbarian's offer?"

"It was definitely interesting, sire. It confirms what we have been told. Do you want me to give the order to go ahead with the plan?"

Kanakore considered this.

"Yes. We will do what our new friend asks and see out his idea," he said, indicating the message in his hand. "And get word to Bradok. He should know better than to fail me."

Covolar nodded and left through a door, hidden in an alcove behind the throne.

Lawrence and Hyperion joined Alex and Thomas in the quarters provided by the King. A meal had been prepared for them and served on the table in the centre of the room. One of their own soldiers remained on guard outside the door.

"So, how do you think that went?" Alex asked Thomas.

"Quite well, I think," he replied. "They heard us out and they are taking time to think about it. That doesn't mean that they will agree, but it is a start."

"Lawrence, how are the troops faring?" asked Alex.

"Their quarters are fine. The same as would be expected at home. They aren't relaxing too much. Most of them still have a deep distrust for the Islanders. A guard will be outside your room at all times."

"And what about the rest of you?"

"Thomas is in the room next door so the guard will keep an eye on that as well at all times. Hyperion and I are with the soldiers."

"Is there anything else we can do to make sure we get the deal?" Alex asked, turning back to Thomas.

"No, I don't think so. The King will talk with his advisor and maybe some of the island chieftains if they are in the city. All we can do is wait until tomorrow and hope he makes the right decision. Now, let's eat."

They began tasting the food at the table. Alex didn't eat much. He felt too nervous and also, he wasn't used to this type of food, mostly fish and unfamiliar spices. Hyperion didn't like it either.

Suddenly, there was a knock at the door. The guard opened it and a servant entered and bowed, a dish in his hands.

"My lord, a gift from the King," he said.

"I don't-" Alex began before Thomas cut him off.

"Thank you. We are grateful. Put it on the table."

The servant placed the dish carefully on the table before backing out of the room.

Alex turned to Thomas once the door was closed.

"I didn't want the food."

"I know. But it is considered very rude on this island to refuse a gift from the King." He lifted the lid of the dish. "And it is a fine gift at that. Sadly, I have already eaten enough. Anyone else want it?"

They all shook their heads.

"So, what shall we do with it?"

Alex thought for a moment.

"Christopher!" he called out. The guard opened the door and looked into the room. "Have you eaten yet?"

"No, my lord," the guard replied.

"Have this then." Alex pointed to the dish. "We don't want it. And there's no need for a guard while these two are already here." He indicated Hyperion and Lawrence, then gestured for Christopher to take a seat.

The next morning, Alex woke up to the door flying open. He came to just as a crossbow bolt hit the man frozen above him in the head. He heard a knife clatter to the floor. He sprang out of bed and reached for his sword then looked towards the door and calmed down. Lawrence stood there gasping for breath, gripping a crossbow in his hand and looking at the dead man.

"What in Gods' name just happened?" demanded Alex.

"I was walking the corridor, coming to check on the guard. I found him dead, his throat slit. So I barged in here to see this man over you. Then I shot him."

"Get the troops ready," ordered Alex. "We have to leave here immediately! Or there might be more."

Lawrence saluted and turned to leave.

"And send Thomas in here!" Alex shouted after him.

Alex quickly got dressed and poured himself a glass of water. His hand shook as he did it. *If Lawrence hadn't been there, I'd be dead,* he thought, looking down at the body of the would-be assassin. He heard a knock at the door and turned around. Thomas bustled in, still in the process of dressing.

"What can you tell me about this?" Alex asked him.

Thomas walked over to the dead man. He was in complete black, from head to toe. Thomas removed the mask to reveal a ruined face. Two scars lined each cheek plus of course the new addition of a crossbow bolt in his head.

"Ah," Thomas said, looking at the face. He picked up the dropped knife. "Ah."

"What? What is it?" Alex asked.

"It is what I expected upon hearing of the attempt. He is a member of The Scirios, the King's Assassins. They are the deadliest killers we know of. They only work on the order of the King of the Islands of Hostiban. The Islanders may be fond of war but they know sometimes the best solution is a knife in the dark. But I thought King Kanakore had disbanded them at the start of his reign some thirty years ago. He believed they had become too powerful."

"Well, apparently he didn't. We have to leave this island."

Lawrence came back into the room, followed by Hyperion. Both had their hands on their weapons.

"Are the soldiers ready?" asked Alex.

"Yes, they're waiting," said Lawrence. "However, one of them is dead."

"What?" Alex was shocked.

"Christopher. It looked like a poisoning."

Alex thought for a second, then looked at them in horror.

"I gave him the gift from the King." Lawrence nodded. "Come on. This is definitely not safe. We must leave as quickly and quietly as possible."

They left the room stealthily and crept silently down the corridor. It opened out into the courtyard where the soldiers were waiting. The guards on the gate had been knocked out and tied up. The gate stood wide open.

Once into the streets, they began running. The sun was just appearing over the horizon. Horns sounded behind them. They quickened their pace, knowing warriors would soon begin pouring out of the palace. As they rounded a corner and rushed onto the quayside, Captain Natalie had already heard the warning horns and lowered the gangplank. Alex sprinted the final distance and ran up the gangplank, the rest of the soldiers behind him.

"Go, go!" he shouted as the plank was pulled back aboard.

Soldiers ran out of the side streets, firing arrows at the ship. Alex's men raised their shields as the ship pulled out of the harbour and headed for the open sea.

Alex joined Thomas in the cabin and sat down.

"We're lucky we got out."

"I know," said Thomas. "They wanted you dead. A lot."

"That will signal an end to our peace," he said with barely concealed anger.

"You know, that has been bothering me. They made such an open attempt on your life. They must have been pretty sure that they would be forgiven for it."

"How?"

"That, I can't figure out."

Meanwhile, King Kanakore paced his room in a rage.

"They what?" he roared.

"They have escaped, sire," said Covolar the Advisor, seated as usual next to the throne. "Left the island on their boat."

"What of the attempt?"

"The assassin is dead. Crossbow bolt to the head. And the poisoned meal was eaten by a guard."

"I've had enough of this. Poisoners, Assassins, Pirates, none of them have succeeded. Get my fastest ships ready. When all else fails, we resort to the old ways."

10: The Return

Alex stepped out on deck and joined Captain Natalie, who was puffing on a pipe and looking intently out to sea, a telescope in one hand. They were due to arrive at the duchies by the end of the day.

"Anything happening, Captain?" he asked.

"Ship's following," she said, drawing on her pipe.

"What?" said Alex, startled. "From the Islands? Where?"

She handed him the telescope and pointed. Alex could just make out in the distance a ship moving towards them and flying the green of the flag of the Islands.

"It's getting closer," he said, alarm in his voice.

"Aye. But it won't catch me, boss. This ship is quick enough when she wants to be. Plus, it ain't in our way and we are almost at the duchy. It ain't gonna go there. It knows it'd lose. No need to worry, boss."

Alex left her and walked over to where Thomas was also staring intently at the ship.

"You've seen our tail?" asked Thomas.

"Yes. Natalie thinks it is no threat."

"But that's not the point. It doesn't make any sense. I mean, the King must really want you dead. Or, he thinks if you are dead, he will gain a lot. But I can't think what that could be. It would surely start a war. He is taking a great many risks. I don't know. War is something they have always done, so he wouldn't care too much if another started. But he is specifically hunting you and I just don't know why."

"Don't worry about it," Alex patted him on his back. "At least it won't catch us. By tonight, we'll be back in safe territory."

Natalie proved to be right. The trailing ship got close but pulled back once they were in sight of the duchy's shore. Alex only breathed easy when they arrived back on dry land where the King wouldn't attack. He led his group to the palace and immediately had an audience with Duke Richard who looked surprised to see them.

"Alexander. We weren't expecting you back so soon. Your trip was successful?"

"Alas, I'm afraid not. The King betrayed us and ordered several attempts on my life."

"I regret to say I'm not surprised," said Richard. "It is the barbarian way. There will never be true peace between us. But if he tried to kill you, then he is ready to end the truce. I will have to step up my ships. Alex," he said in a softer tone. "I'm afraid I have some bad news."

"What is it?"

"A message arrived for you this morning. Your father is sick."

"How bad?" asked Alex, shocked. He thought his father had seemed in good health when he left if a little tired.

"Very bad, it says. He rarely wakes up and can barely move. I'm sorry."

Alex was horrified. He had left his father alone, with only Marcus. *I shouldn't have gone,* Alex thought. *I should never have left my father. He needs me.*

Alex looked up at Richard.

"Go, Alex," Richard said. "Return to your land as quickly as possible."

Alex nodded at the duke and hurried out of the room. Hyperion was waiting with the soldiers and the horses. The Sirona soldiers had already left, apart from Lawrence. Alex said a quick goodbye before mounting and leading those who remained of his group out of the city.

After the first day of riding hard, Alex slowed the group down. He realised he couldn't sprint the whole distance, because the horses wouldn't make it. He was so scared for his father. Alex didn't want him to die. If he did, he would be alone.

A couple of days out from Sirona, Alex was chatting with Thomas and some of the soldiers travelling with him. There wasn't anything else to do on the long miles ahead and Alex wanted to take his mind off his father.

"So, Thomas, what did you think of the Islands? Was it like what you had read?"

"No, sir, not really. We have never really been there, at least not on peaceful terms. All our books talk about them at war and cover nothing else."

"Well, maybe you can add to them now. And you, Joseph?" Alex asked the soldier beside him. "What did you think of it?"

"It was very interesting, my lord. I haven't been to many places outside of Cosando and it was definitely different, sir. I thought-"

Suddenly he stopped speaking and it was replaced by a gurgling sound. Alex looked on in horror as Joseph fell from his horse, with an arrow sticking from his throat.

"Dear Gods," said Alex, staring at the body. Then he shouted out: "We're under attack!"

The soldiers around him immediately began pulling out weapons. A man popped up from behind a rock, a bow in his hand. A soldier swung around and shot him with a crossbow before he could fire. Another three appeared and were dispatched without firing one shot between them.

Alex looked ahead to see a group of riders heading towards them. Back behind them, the same. On either side, sheer rock faces formed a canyon. They were trapped.

Hyperion pulled out his sword and began riding towards the front group. The soldiers followed his lead. When they got nearer, Alex saw they were bare-chested and covered in tattoos. Just like on the Islands. Once in range, the duchy soldiers began firing arrows. And then they collided with the enemy. Alex, trying to keep control of his horse, blocked a spear coming towards him and struck at the wielder. He knew his experience of this type of fighting was limited and wished he'd practised more. He swung his sword around and killed a horse underneath an Islander. The rider leapt off and landed on Alex, pulling him off his horse. They tumbled to the ground together. Alex rolled to his feet first and stabbed the other warrior. He glanced around. The first attacking group had been killed. Only a few of Alex's riders were dead. All the others had been knocked from their horses. Alex walked over to where Hyperion stood, axe bloody in his hand. He was watching the approaching riders.

"I see you're still alive, Al," he said, without looking towards him.

"You seem okay as well, Hyp." Alex looked at the bodies on the floor. "They must have followed us from the Islands. Landed somewhere else."

"Yes. Let's make them pay for entering our land," said Hyperion, grinning as the riders drew closer.

Some of the soldiers around Alex began firing at them. Alex sheathed his sword, picked up a fallen spear and as the warriors neared, hurled it at them. It flew forward and stuck into the lead rider. Alex drew his sword and slashed at another fighter as a horse went past. Rider and horse crashed to the ground. Hyperion beside him was swinging and killing with his axe.

Suddenly, Alex's eyes were drawn to an enemy warrior across the group. As his horse was taken out from under him, he rolled under a swinging sword and killed his opponent with his spear, the only spear amongst his group to be fixed with an iron tip. He swung it around and killed another fighter. He saw Alex watching him and grinned, then pulled his arm back and threw the spear.

Hyperion had been watching him as well. He was the last Islander standing. When Hyperion saw the arm move back, he shoved Alex out of the way and onto the ground. The spear flew across the group and sunk deep into Hyperion's chest. Hyperion looked down at it sticking out of him and fell to the ground.

"NO!!" screamed Alex.

He staggered to his feet, his sword and shield dropping from his hands and ran over to kneel beside Hyperion's fallen body. Hyperion smiled when he saw Alex then closed his eyes for the final time. Alex sobbed. This was his best friend. He had known him his whole life. And he lay dead having taken the blow so Alex could survive. Alex felt rage flow through his veins. He looked around through blurry eyes. The warrior had picked up a wooden spear and had already killed two more soldiers. Alex got to his feet, picking up Hyperion's axe as he did so and charged.

The warrior saw him approaching and grinned. He raised his spear to block the swinging axe. But Alex swung the axe with all his might. It cut right through the spear and into the warrior's chest. The grin fled from his face. He staggered backwards and collapsed to the ground.

Alex bent over the body and looked into the man's eyes.

"Why? Why did you chase me?" Alex asked the rage inside him ebbing away.

The warrior smiled, blood dripping from his mouth.

"I follow the orders of King Kanakore."

"Tell me!"

"A traitor lurks in the shadows. You're already dead, you just don't know it. Hail the Island King!" The man closed his eyes, and his breathing slowed to a stop.

Alex stood up and looked around. Only three soldiers remained alive. Miraculously, Thomas had also survived by keeping out of the way of the onslaught, the enemy soldiers wanting to kill the fighters first. Alex gathered his troops and they buried their fallen comrades. The Islanders' bodies were burned. Alex buried the axe along with Hyperion. Then they found their scattered horses and headed for home.

When he arrived back, Alex asked after his father and was told he was sleeping so he went straight to the throne room, where he found Lord Marcus and General Tyson deep in discussion. They looked up in surprise when Alex came in.

"Alex? You're alive?" said Tyson, his voice filled with surprise and concern.

"Of course, I'm alive. What made you think otherwise?"

"I had hoped you were," said Marcus. "You sent no messages and we all know what those barbarians are like."

"Well, you weren't far wrong."

Alex relayed the whole story of his trip and the ambush on the way back. He had wanted to go straight to his father but he had other tasks first; he was the acting duke until either his father recovered or Bruce returned.

Alexander looked at his father lying on the bed. *He looks so frail*, Alex thought. He hadn't realised how much of a strain the work must have put on him until now. It would have been easier back when he was a young man and the duchess still alive. Alex hadn't realised how much harder life became following his mother's death.

He patted his father's hand and walked over to the table by the window. The game of Drakanimo was still laid out on the board. Alex looked down at the game pieces. He remembered it was his turn. As he moved one of his pieces forward, the room seemed to fall into a strange, unearthly silence. When he turned back, he saw his father was dead. He wept tears of such sorrow, clasping his father's hand again. Then he felt as if pure, cold steel had filled his veins. This had nothing to do with the work of ruling the duchy, his father had been cruelly murdered. Alex vowed that vengeance would be swift.

That night, Alex heard the door of his room click shut and footsteps slowly approach. He smiled grimly and continued his pretence of heavy breathing. He had been expecting this. Ever since the dying warrior's warning, he had tried to work out who the traitor was. And whoever it was, they would try again. He couldn't trust anyone to protect him, so he had prepared himself. His hand under the pillow squeezed the hilt for reassurance.

The footsteps drew closer and stopped. Alex spun his hand around. The hilt caught a person on the side of the face. The would-be murderer crumpled to the floor. Alex crept over to the door and opened it then moved quickly down the hall to the next room, Bruce's room. Inside, two of the three surviving soldiers from the journey to the Islands waited. The third stood guard over his father's body until it was safe to announce the news of his death.

Alex gestured for them to follow him. They were the only ones he trusted not to tell anyone about this. They had wanted to guard his door but Alex had gone against that. He needed the assassin to make an attempt on him, so he could discover his identity. They entered the room and the guards walked over to the man as Alex lit some candles. In the light, Alex could see that the attacker was a young man. He was just coming around as the two soldiers grabbed his arms. He looked in fright at the two of them and then at Alex.

"Please, please, don't kill me," he begged.

"Who sent you?" Alex asked.

"Please, I was only following orders. Don't kill me."

"Answer the questions and I won't kill you."

The man looked at the two guards on either side, gulped and then he whispered a name.

"Are you sure?" Alex couldn't believe it. It was the one person he had never even suspected.

"Yes. I'm sure. Now please, don't kill me."

Alex nodded.

"Lock him in the other room and stay with him. If what he says is true, then we can't let word get out that we've caught him."

The guards dragged him into the other room, as they heard more footsteps running towards them and the third guard entered the room.

Later that day, Alex waited alone in the throne room, standing in front of his father's throne. He turned as Marcus came in.

"Ah, Marcus, thank you for coming."

"It is very early, Alex."

"I know. But some matters can't wait. I have discovered a traitor," he said, watching Marcus' face closely.

"Really, Alex? Who is it?"

"Enough with the games, Marcus. We both know it is you." Alex watched Marcus feign shock.

"Me? You are mistaken! I would never betray you."

"Enough of the lies! You betrayed us!"

Alex saw Marcus put his hand behind his back and got ready. Marcus leapt forward, knife in hand but Alex grabbed the arm before the knife could reach.

"Your family stole the throne from me!" he roared.

Four guards rushed into the room but Alex signalled for them to wait. He wanted to hear Marcus out.

"My grandfather should have had the throne," seethed Marcus. "But he was cast aside for Titus. Why? Because he was a better general and my grandfather made one mistake! The throne should have been mine. Your father deserves the pain I have given him. I shall take the throne!"

Marcus brought his hand back and thrust the knife forward again. Alex blocked it but not before it nicked his cheek. This time the guards seized Marcus.

"Lock him in the deepest dungeon. He has committed treason and murdered the Duke of Cosando."

Marcus looked surprised, then smiled.

"So, the old fool is finally dead."

"I can't execute you Marcus but I can lock you up for a long time."

The guards began dragging Marcus out of the room as Tyson entered and looked on in shock. Suddenly, Marcus stood up straight and pulled forward.

"I wish for the Chance of Royalty."

Everyone gasped.

The Chance of Royalty was an old law. Members of royalty couldn't be executed, only locked up. But the Chance of Royalty allowed any of them to demand an opportunity to free themselves. They would fight the duke's chosen fighter in a duel with neither permitted to kill the opponent. If the accused won, he was set free but had to leave the duchy. If he lost, he faced certain execution. The law had not been invoked in their lifetime.

"Choose your champion, duke. That means-" started Marcus.

"I know what it means," said Alex. "It'll take place in five days. And I shall fight you myself."

11: The Duel

After announcing the death of his father, Alex's day passed in a whirlwind. All the city officials visited to offer their respects and support. Alex was the duke now unless Bruce returned from his adventure. Some long-dead leader had decreed that the duchy couldn't survive without someone in charge for long. So, a law had been written, stating that if the leader died, the next in line currently present in the land, took his place, until anyone else came to claim their legal birthright.

"Are you sure this duel with Marcus is a good idea?" said General Tyson, when they were alone.

"Yes, Tyson. I want to do this," Alex replied. "We must call a council meeting as well. All the dukes should know of the death of my father and the recent events."

"The Council has already been called. It will take place in seven days."

"Good. I will go to it after the duel."

"You don't think this is too big a risk?"

"No. I want my revenge. I will fight him myself."

"Don't forget, he was a soldier in his youth. I remember his speed and prowess as a fighter. Don't underestimate him."

"I shan't," replied Alex grimly. "Now, on to other matters."

Alexander watched as they carried his father's body into the tomb. The minstrels played the sombre song which accompanied the death of a duke. He looked up and away from the crowds of officials to view the surrounding burial grounds. Royal Field lay just beyond the outskirts of the city and the many tombs represented all the dukes who had died whilst ruling this land. Alex looked down through his tears, as his father was finally laid to rest, the latest in his family's long history. Then he felt his shoulders straighten, his head raised and his eyes focus. Tomorrow, the duel with Marcus and his chance to avenge this cruel death.

After the funeral, Alex went directly to his father's room. There, on a stand before him, lay the sword which had been passed down through the centuries from father to son, its origin lost in history. Alex seized it and admired its beauty and magnificence. It felt so light, light enough to be held in one hand but strong enough to deliver powerful blows. A deep red jewel glowed and shone from its setting in the pommel.

Alex swung it around a couple of times, just to get the feel of it. Such a beautiful sword! He remembered that Bruce had never liked it that much. He always preferred two small swords when fighting. But when Bruce became duke, he would have had to take it. *He may never be duke now,* Alex reflected sadly.

The following day, Alex strapped on his armour and tightened it. He smiled at Tyson as he entered the room.

"Good luck, Alex," Tyson said, shaking his hand. "Don't fail."

"I'll try not to. Let's teach this traitor a lesson."

"Remember, Alex, Marcus is tricky. His life is on the line. Don't expect him to play fair. And, when you win, resist the temptation to kill him. You have to execute him the official way. Do not let your emotions cloud you." Tyson patted him on the back before heading out to join the crowd.

Alex picked up his sword and shield and took a deep breath. This was it. He opened the door and walked out into the walled arena.

The arena was small enough, a pit dug into the ground, the surrounding wall at ground level, with a railing to keep spectators back. Its normal use was for training up the palace guard. Nobody could remember the last time it saw this kind of contest. To one side a seating area usually provided a good position for the generals and military personnel to watch the recruits. Today, it was filled with high city officials, along with Tyson and Thomas. More people crowded the length of the railing, eager to see their duke fight a traitor.

Marcus was already waiting in the centre of the arena, wearing full armour, in one hand a shiny new shield and in the other, he gripped his old sword, reclaimed from the wall in the room where it had hung for years. The visor on his helmet was pulled up and he grinned at Alex.

Tyson stood up from his seat. He cleared his throat. The crowd fell silent.

"This is the Chance of Royalty, requested by Lord Marcus of Cosando," he announced. "Duke Alexander of Cosando has chosen to face the claimant himself. Remember," he said, looking at each man. "You are not to kill your opponent."

Tyson raised his hand high and after a pause which seemed to last a lifetime, he brought it down.

"Begin the contest!"

The two fighters slammed their visors shut and readied their swords. They began circling each other. Marcus leapt forward. Alex brought his shield up and blocked the blow. He swung back with his own and encountered a shield. They exchange a brief flurry of blows, each hitting nothing but shield. They backed up and resumed circling.

Marcus made another move. Alex once again brought up his shield but this time Marcus changed his strike mid-swing. The sword crashed into Alex's side forcing him back with the strength of the blow. Marcus swung again. Alex parried the blow with his sword and crashed his shield into Marcus' helmet. Marcus stumbled backwards. Alex advanced on him, swinging his sword. But again and again, it was blocked. Eventually, he backed off, trying to catch his breath.

Alex watched in astonishment as Marcus tossed his shield away, ripped off his helmet and threw it after the shield. He grinned at Alex. A bruise was forming on his cheek where Alex's shield had hit.

"Come on, Alex. Fight me like a true man."

Alex knew he shouldn't. Marcus was a better fighter and this would give him an advantage. He knew this was a trick but he didn't care. Anger boiled through his veins. If Marcus wanted to fight this way, he would fight. He threw away his shield and took off his helmet. All the time, Marcus just stood there, grinning at him. Alex's hair was covered in sweat. They began circling again.

Marcus stepped forward and rained blows down onto Alex. Alex parried with his sword but each blow had power behind it. Marcus kept going, as Alex's arms grew weaker, no longer succeeding in his attacks, just barely able to block. Then Alex remembered the stories of Marcus' military career. With one kick, he cracked into his opponent's knee and Marcus staggered backwards, the old arrow wound suddenly in agony. Alex swung his sword, striking Marcus' gauntlet, causing him to drop his sword and fall to his knees. He tore his gauntlet off to relieve the pain of his crushed fingers. He looked up too late.

The tip of Alex's sword was pressed into his neck. He looked up into Alex's eyes. The crowd cheered.

"Kill me," Marcus growled. "Do it. Kill me now and spare the hangman his job."

Alex knew it would be so easy. No-one would care. Marcus was a self-confessed traitor. He looked up at the crowd and saw Tyson staring back at him. Alex thought of his father; what he would have done. He lowered his sword.

"No."

"KILL ME!" Marcus roared.

"No. You aren't worth it," Alex turned and began walking away.

"You coward!" screamed Marcus.

Suddenly he was on his feet pulling a knife hidden beneath his belt. He leapt at Alex's turned back, aiming at the exposed neck. Alex had been expecting this. He knew Marcus' tricks. He turned swiftly on his heel, swinging his sword. The knife flew away from Marcus, the hand still closed around it.

Marcus looked down at the stump at the end of his arm, blood spurting from it into the dust of the arena. He began screaming. Two guards arrived and swiftly carried him away. Tyson ordered them to take him to the medic before going to his cell. Alex wiped the blood from his blade.

The next day, Alex prepared to leave for the Council of the Dukes in the fallen city of Regnor. The Council was set to take place in three days and Alex needed all that time just to reach there. Thomas, some clerks and a small regiment of soldiers would accompany him. General Tyson remained to deal with the running of the duchy and strengthen the war defences.

They hanged Marcus that morning. Alex did not choose to witness it, his memories of Marcus still fresh enough in his mind. He heard the execution drew a large crowd. Hangings were rare these days. All of the duchies thought they had progressed beyond such remedies. However, in this case, Alex knew they had no choice. Now, he just felt relieved that the threat of treason had been dealt with.

Alex instructed Tyson to send a message to King Kanakore. If Marcus was the reason why he had refused to help them, then maybe with Marcus gone, the Islands could send some troops. This came as a suggestion from Thomas and Alex agreed it was worth a shot.

As Alex set out, he looked forward to a meeting with the other dukes. They were all older than him, some the same age as his late father. They had had years of experience between them and he would value their opinion on how to deal with the goblins. He needed help and these leaders could surely provide it.

***

Captain Howard of Gultrum Outpost watched as the goblins entered the clearing surrounding the tower. This was not the first attack, yet there seemed more this time than before and certainly more organised. He realised he had almost been expecting this, what with the new information they had discovered earlier. It made sense to any military mind. He hadn't had time to write the letter to Cosando before this group arrived.

He gathered his archers at the main room of the tower and sent them out to different windows. They would be the first line of defence. He watched as a massive goblin emerged from between the trees. He had been warned about these. It was what General Tyson had described as an officer goblin.

Captain Howard surveyed the rest of the troops. He knew he didn't have the numbers to withstand a coordinated attack. It wouldn't stop him trying, though. He had been a soldier all his life and fought in many battles. He always knew that the next one could be the last. It was what his family had always done, fighting wars, first for the kings and then the dukes.

He returned to the top of the tower where the last messenger bird was sleeping in a cage. They kept enough supplies here to sustain soldiers waiting for reinforcements to arrive; food, water, lamps, lamp oil, arrows and other vital items stored in wooden boxes. Howard knew that no amount of supplies would keep him here long enough for reinforcements to fight their way through the goblin horde. Not with the new knowledge he had.

The assault on the tower had begun by the time Howard stood up behind the parapets to watch. The officer goblin commanded them to break down the door. Others held their shields over the breakers to protect them from arrow fire. Archer goblins positioned themselves around the edge of the clearing, firing at Howard's troops in the windows. Many cougars wandered in and out of the goblin torches, waiting, sensing a meal was near. More goblins rode in on the backs of cougars and dismounted ready for the fight.

Captain Howard turned and began writing a message to the Duke as the door creaked far below him. He was still writing when he heard it shatter. Outside the tower, some cougars took advantage of the lapse in concentration of Howard's archers and leapt up to climb in the lower windows.

Howard walked over to the bird and calmly tied the message to its leg, before setting it loose. He could hear the screams of his squad dying below him, as well as the snarls of the cougars and the cackles of excitement from the goblins. He opened the crates marked 'Lamp Oil' and began pouring it all over the floor and down the hatch. He was grateful for the wooden floors of this building. He had emptied three cases of bottles of the liquid before hearing sounds of goblins climbing up the ladder towards him. He calmly struck a couple of matches and dropped them onto the floor and down the hatch.

As the watchtower turned into an inferno below him, ending the lives of both the enemy creatures and his own men, Captain Howard remembered his ancestors who had fought and died for the land. He wondered if his own son could hope to break free from this tradition.

12: The Council

Alexander and his party entered Regnor City by the main gate. The guards, who represented all the duchies, let them through swiftly. After the fall of the last King, Regnor had fallen into chaos. No duchy claimed ownership so there was no leader. Most residents fled to other cities. Houses were ransacked and looted, but the palace guards stayed. Eventually, an agreement was reached. All duchies sent troops to protect the city and the palace from any further bandits. By then, there were no citizens left and none ever came back.

It had been years since Alex had been here. The dukes normally met officially once a year, to discuss political matters and trade deals. When Alex was younger, he had accompanied his father to most of these but in later years his father had attended alone.

Alex's group arrived at the palace and the servants took the horses to be stabled. Alex looked around and noted by the soldiers' various uniforms that most of the dukes were already present.

"Sire," a bird keeper said, as they entered the palace. "Are you the Duke of Cosando?"

"Yes. What is it?" Alex asked.

"A message arrived for you this morning, Your Grace."

He handed him two pieces of paper before hurrying away. Alex looked down at them. One was from Gultrum Outpost, the other from General Tyson. He unfolded the one from the outpost. It read:

'My Lord Duke, I send you disturbing news. Gultrum Outpost has fallen. We were attacked by goblins and cougars. All my troops are dead but let it be remembered that they died fighting. Some information was discovered today, that I will now pass on to you.

'The news, sir, concerns an enemy army. We have spotted signs of goblins gathering, planning, preparing. Vast numbers have come over the mountains. We believe you will be attacked within the next two weeks. I hope you prepare the best you can. I wish you the best of luck. Your servant to the very end,

Captain Howard.'

Alex wordlessly handed it over for Thomas to read. He opened the one from Tyson, it was brief.

'I have read the message, Your Grace. Our army is gathering at the Pass. We will be ready. Tyson.'

Alex passed that one over as well. This was seriously bad news. At least they had received prior warning of the attack. Without it, the Pass would have been destroyed. Fortunately, Tyson had stayed behind and could now command the duchy's defence.

"The news is bad, Thomas," said Alex.

"Aye, it is very bad," replied Thomas. "But there's nothing more we can do from here but tell the dukes. We will need their support to deal with this."

"You're right," said Alex. "Let's go."

Guards pushed the doors open to the Council Room as Alex approached. He entered into a grand hall, once the throne room for the kings of old. The throne had been replaced with a large, round table filling the centre of the space. Eight chairs had been positioned around it, one for each duke or duchess. Benches lined the edge of the room for advisors and heirs to sit in and take note of decisions. Light penetrated from windows high above and a chandelier hung above the table.

The other leaders of the duchies had already claimed their seats and were talking to each other or their advisors. Everyone fell quiet as Alex walked over to the final chair. He stood behind it for a moment before speaking.

"Duke Philipp of Cosando, son of Duke Titus, is dead."

The other dukes listened incredulously.

"My brother, Lord Bruce, is missing, presumed dead. I am Duke of Cosando now."

Alex sat down in his chair.

"How did Philipp pass away? From the sickness?" asked Duke Richard.

"Yes and no. He died from the sickness but no natural one. He was poisoned by Lord Marcus, his advisor."

"Marcus? I knew Marcus. I didn't think him capable of such treachery."

"Neither did we, Richard," said Alex sadly. "Neither did we."

"And Bruce? Wasn't he sent on some mission to defeat the creatures?" asked another duke.

"Yes. We have received no news of him and the creatures still come. We suspect the worst."

"This is disturbing news you carry with you, Alex," said the only duchess at the table.

"There is more. I have just received word from my outpost beyond the Pass. They say an army is approaching."

"When will it arrive?" asked the third duke.

"We have less than a fortnight. My army is already gathering at the Pass."

"That is hardly any time to prepare!" said the fourth.

"It will have to do."

"What can we do in that time?"

"Most of us can't get troops there in that time," said the duchess.

"My soldiers can," said the third. "At least a portion of them anyway."

"Thank you, Duke Lewis," said Alex. "Any troops will be greatly appreciated."

"What about the rest of us?" asked the fourth.

"We will get ready," said the one duke who hadn't spoken so far, after a moment of silent thought.

He was the oldest and had ruled for a long time. He had been a young duke when the last King was thrown down and the only duke still alive in power then. Only Alex's father and one other duke had even been born then.

"We will send our troops there when we can. Alexander's soldiers will have to do the best they can until we arrive. His grandfather held that pass for many days before reinforcements arrived. We will gather all our armies together, and then we shall crush the enemy."

"Thank you, Duke Frederick," said Alex. "We will hold the Pass for as long as we can. However, be warned that we are facing no ordinary army. These are not humans. These are goblins. They are fiercer than most humans and know nothing of mercy. They have already completely destroyed the Empire. We can't let the same happen here."

After another prolonged discussion, the Council broke up and Alex said he must leave without delay.

As he prepared to mount his horse, he saw Duke Lewis hurrying towards him, with a woman by his side. After the Council, all the dukes were hastening to depart. The messenger birds had been very busy with warnings dispatched to the duchies to ready the troops. Alex had got Thomas to send one to Tyson explaining the outcome of the Council. Now, they had to hurry back to help in the war preparations.

"Duke Lewis, I want to thank you for your support," said Alex as Lewis arrived.

"Glad to help, Alex," Lewis said. "I've sent instructions back to ready the army. I want to introduce you to someone. This is my daughter, Lady Elizabeth. She will be leading my troops."

Alex turned to the woman next to the duke and had to force himself not to stare. He had met Elizabeth a couple of times when they were younger but it must have been twenty years since he had last seen her. And he definitely didn't recall her looking like this. He remembered a small, shy girl who rarely left her parents' side. In front of him now stood a tall, stunning woman with luxurious black hair cascading down to her shoulders. She looked more like a warrior than Alex himself. Alex realised he had failed at not staring and quickly looked away.

"Hi Alex," she said, smiling brightly. "Nice to see you again."

"Um, hello. Good to, um, see you too," he replied, but later wasn't sure if he had even been as coherent as that. She didn't seem to notice.

"Well, I have to get going but I'll see you again in a couple of days," she said, flashing him a final smile before turning and walking away, leaving Alex staring speechlessly after her.

"Come on. We have to go," said Thomas, grabbing his arm.

"Yes, yes. I'm coming."

He kept watching until she turned a corner and vanished from his sight. Then he shook his head as if to clear his thoughts, hopped up onto his horse and led his group out of the palace and the city. They had to get back to Cosando as fast as humanly possible.

The image of Elizabeth standing there stayed in Alex's mind for the rest of the day. It was the first time in weeks he had thought about something other than the goblins and his family.

13: The Pass

Alexander arrived at the Pass of Titus and saw the gathered troops. He had ridden hard with his group to get here in five days. Thomas had stayed behind in Cosando City to see to it that all ran smoothly while Alex was away. Here at the Pass, almost all the troops of Cosando were gathered. A small number had been left to guard the city and some of the towns but all others were here.

General Tyson walked over to Alex as soon as the horses were stabled.

"Glad to see you finally got here, Your Grace," said Tyson as they shook hands. Alex smiled.

"Got here as fast as I could. I see you have been busy."

"Yes, I have. Most of the troops were able to get here quickly enough, but I don't know how long we can hold the Pass for."

"You got my message? About Duke Lewis' troops from Mirando?"

"Yes and I'm glad. We'll need all the troops we can get."

"The others will arrive soon."

"Let's just hope there is someone here to greet them. Someone other than the goblins. Now, I'll show you the plan." Tyson turned and entered the fort.

The Pass was a narrow gap between two mountains, only wide enough for ten riders abreast. At the Cosando entrance, a stone fortress had been built across the gap. A portcullis at this fort could be lifted to let riders through, as well as a small side door, to allow in small numbers of people. On either side of the

Pass, a ledge had been dug out. Archers would be situated up there to shoot down on enemy troops. At the Empire side of the ledges, walls had been built to protect the archers. The walls of the Pass were entirely smooth so no one could climb up. The Pass presented an effective defence for the people of the duchies, against the threat of invaders from the North. The only other access to them on land was via treacherous mountain passes, which couldn't support a large army. The alternative for an enemy would be to build a fleet and sail around the rocky coast.

Tyson's plan for this defence was simple and based on similar methods used successfully in the past. Archers would be stationed on both ledges, with more waiting in the fort, to relieve the others when they got tired. Down below, soldiers would be stationed in front of the fort to stop the goblins from having a chance at destroying the gate. Same as the archers, more soldiers would be waiting in the fortress. Tyson would be on the ledges with the archers, while Alexander would be with the ground troops. Now, they just had to wait and prepare the warriors the best they could.

Alex was outside practising when the messenger ran up. It was a day since he had arrived at the Pass. Ever since Bruce had left and war looked imminent, Alex had trained every day. He missed training with Hyperion. They had always had fun. Ever since his friend's death, Alex had practised fighting with more deadly intent. He had just knocked the sword out of his opponent's hand when the messenger arrived.

"My Lord Duke, Lady Elizabeth of Mirando has arrived with her soldiers."

"Tell General Tyson to come to the main tent, and ask Lady Elizabeth as well," replied Alex immediately.

Alex walked over to his own tent as the messenger ran off. He changed into better clothes before going to the main one. Tents were dotted all around the fields behind the Pass, places for the soldiers to sleep in. They had light canvases and were easily constructed and deconstructed when the army moved. In the centre stood a large pavilion, the headquarters for all major decisions.

When Alex arrived, he found Tyson studying a scale model of the Pass, displayed on a large table in the centre of the pavilion. Alex turned back to the entrance as the herald came in, followed by Lady Elizabeth.

"The Lady Elizabeth of Mirando," announced the herald, before turning and leaving.

"Lady Elizabeth, I'm glad you have arrived in time," said Alex, feeling himself blushing.

He had not forgotten what she looked like in the days that had passed. He coughed and continued.

"Um, this is General Tyson of the army of Cosando."

"It's a pleasure to meet you, my lady," said Tyson, bowing low.

Elizabeth nodded and smiled at him.

"So, Alex, what's the plan?" she asked, turning her smile on him.

"Um, well, it's General Tyson's plan. He will explain it," said Alex. He realised he wasn't used to pretty ladies smiling at him.

"Well, my lady, if you would care to step over here," said Tyson, leading her over to the model of the Pass.

He explained what they expected to happen. He indicated where each squad of troops would be and how they would operate. Eventually, Tyson fell silent and Elizabeth continued studying the model. Finally, she looked up.

"Good plan," she said, looking back to Alex. "I'll be down at the front of the Pass."

"Are you sure, my lady?" asked Tyson, looking from her to Alex and back again.

"Yes. Are you going to try to stop me?" she asked, grinning at him.

"Of course not, my lady."

"Good. I shall go and tell my commanders of the plan."

She gave a final smile at both men, before striding out.

"Impressive woman," said Tyson after she had left. Alex nodded. "Glad she's on our side. Plus, her troops are welcome."

"How many soldiers do we have now?" asked Alex.

"Two thousand of our own plus she brought five hundred with her."

"Let's hope it's enough," said Alex almost to himself.

Later that day, Alex heard a horn sound and immediately went out to investigate. A messenger ran up to him.

"My Lord Duke, the goblins have been spotted," she said.

"Thank you. Make sure the commanders know."

Alex set off for the fortress, stopping at his tent to grab his gear.

He arrived at the Pass to find everyone at a state of readiness. Tyson headed up the stairs to the ledges, nodding to Alex as he went past. Alex walked through the open gate and out to see to his soldiers. Archers lined the ledges on either side.

Elizabeth was already there. She was in full armour with a longsword by her side. She saw him and walked over.

"Are you ready, Alex?" she asked.

"As I'll ever be," he replied. He glanced over at her. "You sure you want to do this?"

"I wouldn't miss it for anything," she said, grinning wickedly and drawing her long sword. "Wouldn't like to let you boys have all the fun, now, would I?"

The horn sounded again. Alex looked ahead to see the lead goblins enter the far end of the clearing. They were mounted on cougars and approaching at speed.

"Spearmen to the front!" he commanded, while someone handed him a spear. "Shields ready!" A shield wall was formed in front of the spearmen. "Get ready!"

"Archers! Ready!" Alex heard Tyson call out above him. "Fire!"

Arrows rained down on the mounted goblins, slaying many. But some made it to the shield wall, riding over the bodies of their comrades. Shields buckled under the weight of their onslaught. Troops thrust their spears forward, killing more goblins and cougars but still more came to take their place.

Behind the cavalry came the main bulk of the goblin horde. The shield wall fell. Swords replaced spears. Hundreds of goblins perished but still more pushed forward, beating down Alex's forces. He saw his own men fall, soldier after soldier, replaced by more from within the fortress. Comrades carried the bodies of friends back inside. Wave after wave crashed upon the forces led by Alex and Elizabeth, yet they stayed standing, stayed fighting. Archers above rained destruction upon their enemies but at a cost. Enemy archers had taken up positions among the foot soldiers below and struck back. But Tyson continued anticipating the enemy, kept issuing commands, shouting orders, changing positions.

Alex stood there, at the front, the whole time, fighting back the goblins. But he was growing tired. Suddenly, an officer goblin appeared in front of him and swung its spear down. Alex raised his shield and blocked the blow but the shield was wrenched from his hand and flung away. The goblin swung its leg up and Alex stumbled to the ground under the force of the kick. The goblin raised its spear for a final thrust but just then, a sword appeared poking out from its chest. It fell forward to reveal Elizabeth standing behind it.

She smiled down at Alex as she gave him a hand up. Alex picked up a shield and as Elizabeth reached down to retrieve her sword from the officer's chest, an arrow flew from deep within the goblin ranks heading straight for Elizabeth. She had no time to move. Suddenly, Alex's shield appeared in front of her and caught the full impact of the arrow. She turned around to see Alex's shield in front of her with the arrow embedded in it. Now it was Alex's turn to smile at Elizabeth. They both turned back to the fight.

Tyson strode among his archers, replacing those that were too tired to continue. The battle had lasted hours and yet there seemed no end to the goblins. He just had to keep switching his archers, trying to keep as many as he could alive and refreshed. He was walking back towards the fortress when he heard a growl above him. He looked up quickly and saw many cougars creeping down the side of the mountain towards them.

"Up above!" he yelled.

But he wasn't quick enough. Cougars along both sides of the Pass pounced on the archers below them. A few managed to pull out their swords but even then, did not survive for long.

Tyson, sword already in hand, fought back. He sliced through the first cougar and dodged a second, watching it fly over the edge and onto the goblins' blades below. More troops poured out of the fortress onto the ledge to fight back the cougars. But Tyson was surrounded. He stabbed another two before one scraped a claw across his side. He stumbled. Another leapt on him pushing him backwards. Together they tumbled onto the goblins.

Alex had looked up at the first shout and had seen his troops being slaughtered. He watched Tyson fight the cougars around him and looked on in horror as he fell over the edge.

"Tyson!" he yelled, trying to get forward.

But the goblins kept pushing onwards. They were using the death of the archers to their advantage. Alex and his troops were being pushed back. More cougars with goblins on them arrived on the ledges. Alex knew his army was lost.

Without warning, two creatures landed in balls of light on either ledge, among the cougars. They were both wielding blades and one had a powerful tiger fighting alongside it. They swiftly slew all the cougars on the ledges. Then they jumped down onto the goblins. Confusion spread among the goblin ranks. These creatures killed easily, piling up the goblin bodies. The ones at the back turned and ran. The ones near the fortress ran straight into the waiting blades of Alex's soldiers. Within minutes, any surviving goblins had fled the Pass and could be seen retreating into the distance. A cheer went up from the surviving soldiers. The warrior who had the tiger by its side looked at them.

"This is only the beginning," he said, his voice carrying across the battlefield.

14: The Slayers

Alexander had never felt such exhaustion in his life. He sat in the main tent, listening to the commanders' reports of the fallen. After the battle, the two creatures and their tiger had left to hunt down surviving goblins before Alex could talk to them. He hadn't even got a good look at them. All they had requested were two horses and said they would arrive at the capital city in a couple of days, to talk to Alex. Also, they informed everyone they were only a scouting party, a bigger army would follow, when they didn't know.

Alex felt too tired to dwell on this. They had lost so many warriors in the battle. He dismissed the commanders when they finished, telling them to see to the burials of the dead. Two mounds would be created for the soldiers of Cosando and Mirando.

Alex missed Tyson already. He had always known how to deal with these things. Tyson's body had been found on the battlefield. Alex had seen to it that he would get his own grave and would be remembered along with the others for the sacrifices they had made.

"What do we do now?" he asked Elizabeth, also present at the meeting.

"Whatever we can," she replied. "We will have to move the troops back. We can't hold this Pass for long, today has proven that. Especially not against a bigger force. The numbers have no end. You were right, these are a lot worse than any humans."

"What about these creatures that just suddenly dropped out of the sky? Who are they?"

"I don't know. We will have to wait until they come to Cosando City."

"What if they are evil?"

"It can't be much worse. They did kill all the goblins." She walked over and patted him on the back. "Get some rest. You've had a long day, with many more to come."

"Yeah, I will." He stood up and stretched. "Thanks, Elizabeth. You fought well today."

"Thank you, Alex. And, please, call me Liz." She smiled at him and walked out of the tent.

The following day, Alexander, Elizabeth and a small retinue of soldiers from both duchies headed for Cosando City. The rest of the surviving troops were split up. Some stayed to guard the Pass, others returned to the other two fortresses, the rest followed Alex back to Cosando where eventually they would join with the armies of the other duchies. Alex had promoted Captain Edward to General as a successor to Tyson and he led the main contingent of troops back to Cosando.

Alex arrived at Cosando to cheers from the waiting crowd. Word had flown ahead of them about their victory at the Pass. Alex led his group through the streets and up to the palace quickly. The people were so glad of the victory but they didn't realise that this wasn't the end. He quickly stabled his horse before heading to the throne room.

Thomas was there waiting for him. He smiled when he saw Alex and Liz enter.

"I'm glad to see you are uninjured, My Lord Duke," he said, bowing.

"So am I, Thomas," replied Alex. "You know Lady Elizabeth?"

"Yes, I do. My lady," he bowed. She nodded back at him.

"You heard about Tyson?" asked Alex.

"Yes, sir. It is a shame. He was a great man and a great general. He will be missed."

"Yes. Now more than ever," said Alex, taking his seat on the throne. "What do you make of these creatures that helped us?"

"I don't know, sir. We just have to hope that they are on our side and arrive here soon."

"The sooner the better. They say another army is coming." Alex sighed. "Any more news here?"

"Not much, sir. The armies from Mirando and Sovano should arrive tomorrow. Both Duke Lewis of Mirando and Duke Henry of Sovano will come themselves."

"My father is coming? Why?" asked Liz.

"Well, you know the dukes, my lady. They don't like to feel that they are left out of important situations. I expect all the dukes will come themselves, though very few are young enough to fight." Thomas turned back to Alex. "There are a few other matters I should discuss with you, sir."

Alex spent the rest of the day catching up on problems he had missed in his absence.

The two dukes arrived the next day, with their armies at their backs. The land in front of the city became filled with tents, as far as the eye could see. The dukes themselves stayed in the spare rooms in the palace. They were informed of all that had happened at the battle and they discussed how best to move forward. The people were no longer celebrating, as the news went around that the war wasn't over.

The day after that, the two creatures and their tiger arrived at the palace. Alex was in a discussion with the other dukes, Thomas, Elizabeth and others who were important officials in the city when the door opened and they simply walked into the throne room. Somehow, they had managed to bypass all the guards at the gates and throughout the palace. Alex sat up and stared at them as they came in. Everyone fell silent.

"We have returned, as promised," said the one in front.

It was the first real chance Alex had to look at them. The one who had spoken was tall and had a very elegant face. He had long pointed ears. Black hair came down to his shoulders. He was in full, pale blue armour with a double-bladed sword at his side. The one behind him looked more like an ordinary man, except for his armour. It was made of the same superior quality as the man's next to him, although his was green coloured. He had a sword in a sheath and a round shield on his back. The tiger beside them looked huge, as big as any horse and sabre teeth glinted either side of its mouth.

"Who are you?" asked Alex, after looking at them for a moment.

But Father Zeno had already stepped forward. He had been invited to these discussions out of respect, even though it was outside his expertise and he didn't have much to offer.

"My Lord Duke, do you not know who these people are?" he asked, looking horrified.

Alex shook his head, as did everyone else in the room.

"These are the Slayers for the Gods, fighters of evil." He turned to the creatures, bent down on one knee and held up his ceremonial staff in front of him. "My lords, I am a humble servant of the Gods. I apologise for my master's lack of understanding of who you are."

"Why don't you explain it to him, then, Father?" asked the one in blue armour, smiling.

Zeno rose and turned back to Alex.

"Your Grace, if I may, I would like to discuss the origin of these people from the very beginning."

"Go on," said Alex, nodding.

"At the beginning of time, there was only the Garden," Zeno started. He had been talking about these things all his life and he knew how to tell this story. "And then the Gods appeared. Twelve Gods. Six Lords and six Ladies. The Gentry, they are often called. They lived in the Garden in harmony with each other. And then the Darkness came. The Thirteenth God. The Abominable Power. The Gods fought this Darkness for an indeterminable amount of time, as time didn't exist yet. Eventually, the Gods succeeded. But they couldn't kill this Darkness. Instead, they banished him. But to banish him, there had to be somewhere other than the Garden and so, with a bang, the Universe of the Gentry was created and time started.

"The Gods joined together to create worlds. Each pair took one of the six necessary parts of worlds. Land, Sky, Water, Forests, Underground and the Afterlife. They each created a people as well. And all was good.

"But then the Darkness returned. He had minions that he sent to conquer planets. These minions used creatures, such as the goblins facing us, to fight for them. So the Gods decided they needed something of their own to combat this. And from that decision came the Slayers. Slayers have armour and weapons created by the Gods themselves, trained by them too. They are the greatest fighters in the Universe. The twelve first Slayers, called the Ancients, were the best of the best. They were trained at the hands of the Gods, rather than by older slayers.

Not many of the Ancients are still around. But there are many Slayers. They spend their lives hunting down the minions of the darkness. And they live for eternity." Zeno fell silent, waiting to see what Alex would do next.

"And you are Slayers, then?" asked Alex after a few minutes of silent contemplation. The one in blue nodded. "Well, I have to say, we do need you."

"More than you know," said the one in blue.

"And who are you?"

"I am Vrisatore Penadoon, Slayer for the Sky," he replied, then pointed to the one behind him. "This is my Apprentice, Rinatore Diabaven, Slayer for the Land. And this," he gestured towards his sabre-tooth tiger. "Is Rumdam."

"I welcome you to Cosando and hope you can help us with our problem."

"We will do what we can."

"Then, what can you tell us about what we are facing?"

"The master here is called Diabolous. He is a true monster. He tortures people for fun and he takes his time corrupting lands. He likes the people to think they have a chance before he destroys them. We have been hunting him for a long time and this is the closest we ever have been. He uses goblins, as most of them do, but on top of that, he uses dead warriors. He has a way of bringing back the souls of the dead and creating bodies for them."

"How come there have been no reports of these dead soldiers, then?" asked Thomas.

"They will only go far from their base when the main army comes or a trick is needed. That's how we know that the army you defeated the other day was only a scouting party, made to test your defences."

"And can we defeat this army?" asked Duke Henry.

"No. Not in a battle. You may win the first battle, or the second but every time one of your soldiers dies, they come back on his side, in addition to all the warriors he already has."

"Then what can we do?" asked Duke Lewis.

"The only way to win is to kill him. Without him, the army will crumble and the dead will return to where they are meant to be."

"And how do we kill him?" asked Alex.

"We wait. We defeat any small army he sends at us. He will come with the main army and when he does, my Apprentice and I will kill him."

"So all we can do is wait?"

"No. On our hunt of the fleeing goblins, we found out about another army. It is going to creep around the East side of the mountains using ships. It consists solely of dead soldiers. It is a feint, a trick to draw off some of our forces and tire us out. But we will have to deal with it."

"Then we must send troops!" said Duke Henry. "That is my duchy they will land in and most of our troops are here."

"Of course, Henry, we will send soldiers," said Alex.

"You won't need many," said Vrisatore. "You just need enough to sink the boats before they can land. We will go ourselves to help oversee these matters."

"I'll go too," said Alex immediately.

“Are you sure, My Lord Duke?” asked Thomas. “Won’t we need you here?”

“No, Thomas, I am sure you’ll be fine. The enemy army won’t be here for a couple of weeks if the Slayers here didn’t see any sign of them. General Edward will be able to keep the army in training. I want to see these dead warriors for myself. I will take a small group of our soldiers.”

“I will send soldiers too,” said Duke Henry. “A Captain of mine will go with you as you are going to my duchy.”

Alex nodded his agreement.

“I must send warriors as well,” said Duke Lewis, realising he hadn’t offered anything yet. “Elizabeth will be glad to take some troops and go with you.”

“So, it is settled,” said Alex. “We will each send one hundred troops. Should that be enough?” He turned back to Vrisatore.

“That should be plenty,” he said, nodding. “However, we may need some ships as well.”

“Send a message to Duchess Victoria of Livona, Thomas,” Alex said, after a moment of thought. “She should be able to send some ships from her island. Good. We must leave tomorrow and make haste.”

***

“Do it. Kill him,” commanded Diabolous.

Bruce looked at the sword he had been given and then back to the man in front of him. The man was whimpering on the floor, blood spilling from the lashes in his back. The goblin behind him was cleaning the blood off his whip. Bruce dropped the sword.

"Really? You still will not kill him? Interesting. Even though it will clearly end his pain and yours? Very interesting. Alright, see what another five lashes will do."

Bruce fell to his knees as the whip landed on his back. He could see the prisoner receiving the same treatment. The whip landed, again and again, raising fresh wounds. When they stopped, Diabolous walked over to the prisoner and stared down at him.

"Oh. It seems they have killed him. Oh, well. There are always more. Guards, take away this body. All of you, leave me."

Bruce watched them drag the torn body out of the door.

"Now, Bruce, what will I do with you? It has been many weeks and still, you try to hold out. It really is quite intriguing. You have lasted longer than anyone else. Sadly, I must stop this experiment. I am at war, you know. So, you must die now."

Without another word, Diabolous picked Bruce up and thrust his spear through him, then threw the limp body onto the floor and took a seat on his throne. He waited.

A while later, Bruce strode into the throne room, wearing full armour, his two swords in sheaths at his side. He walked straight over his former body and knelt before Diabolous.

"Are you ready to fight?" asked Diabolous.

"Yes, Master!"

"Are you ready to kill the humans?"

"Yes, Master!"

"Good. The dead shall march over the mountains and destroy the duchies. You will lead them."

"Yes, Master!"

"One final move and the humans will fall to my unstoppable forces. Prepare the troops for our departure."

"Yes, Master!" Bruce saluted and left the room.

15: The Fleet

Alexander saw it was getting late and called the contingent of warriors to a halt. The soldiers quickly got fires going and set up camp for the night. They were a day away from the coast now. From what Alex could gather from the Slayers, their group should arrive before the ships of the dead. The Slayers kept mostly to themselves but tonight they sat around the fire with Alex, Elizabeth and Captain Graham of Sovano.

"So, where do you get your names from?" asked Alex, trying to learn more about them.

"Our first names we get when we begin our apprenticeship," said Vrisatore. Rumdam was lying up near the fire beside him. "The Lord and Lady we follow give us our name. They all end in 'atore' for males and 'isore' for females to show we are warriors. Apart from the wizards. Theirs end in 'inos' to show they are wise. Our last name shows our status. It is made of the first minion of darkness you killed followed by 'adoon' for Masters. For Apprentices, it is the minion you are hunting followed by 'aven'."

"So, after we succeed here, I will be called Diabadoon instead of Diabaven," said Rinatore. "To show that I killed Diabolous."

"How do you become Slayers?" asked Alex. Father Zeno had told him a little about them before he left but he was curious to find out more.

"Every five years a hundred are chosen from across the Universe," said Vrisatore. "After five years of training, they become Apprentices. But by that time there are only twenty-four of the original hundred left, the others having failed or quit.

The Apprentices join a Master and travel with him or her until they kill a minion. Normally they try to give Apprentices to Masters of the same branch, you know, give a Human Apprentice to a Human Master. But obviously, with us, there were no Human Masters around so I had to take Rinatore. Not all Apprentices become Masters though. Some die, others never kill the minion they are chasing, and some give up."

"We have been chasing Diabolous for a couple of decades now," said Rinatore. "It will be nice to finally kill him. We have seen the damage he has done, the planets he has destroyed and it will be good for him to finally receive justice."

"Speaking of which, what is our plan for these ships?" asked Liz.

"Is there a fort at the coast?" asked Vrisatore, turning to Captain Graham.

"Yes, sir, there is," he replied.

"Does it have siege weapons? Machines that could destroy ships? Catapults and the like?"

"Yes, sir, I would think so. They are pretty standard around the coast."

"Good, good. Then the plan is as follows."

They stayed up late into the night perfecting his ideas.

Alex watched the ships sail around the headland and knew the time had arrived to begin the assault. They had been waiting two days at the fort and the men were growing restless. He was glad the battle was finally here. However, the ships from Livona hadn't arrived yet. Alex just hoped they would come in time. He looked back at the fort behind him. The fire had been lit, signalling the ships had been sighted.

He turned back to the sea. A fleet of ships sailed towards him. He heard a creak as the siege weapons were prepared.

"READY!" shouted Captain Graham. "FIRE!"

The catapults launched their loads of flaming rocks at the incoming fleet. The first ship received a few hits but the rest of the projectiles fell short. The remaining vessels sailed onwards around the sinking remains of their sister ship. They sped up, knowing the siege weapons couldn't hit them if they were too close. Alex could now just make out the warriors aboard, loading their bows and waiting, calmly.

"Get ready!" Alex shouted, looking at the rows of archers behind him. The ships were entering range. "Flame arrows!" All arrows were dipped into the fires beside them. "Aim!" The archers readied themselves. "Fire!" A stream of arrows hurtled against the ships. Another one sank.

The catapults launched again, taking down a ship at the back. Two ships were now in too close a range. It was time for the hand-to-hand fighting. He looked at the rope Vrisatore handed him. A wooden horizontal bar had been constructed out over the water in front of them just for this purpose. He grinned nervously over at Elizabeth and waited for Vrisatore's call. Rumdam paced back and forth around them, waiting for any warriors to try and escape the ships.

"Swing!" shouted Vrisatore.

They all jumped forward and let go of the ropes when they were over the ships. Alex and Liz landed on the nearest boat with a dozen soldiers, while Vrisatore and Rinatore alone landed on the second.

Alex ducked a sword as he hit the deck and pulled out his own sword and shield. He blocked another attack and thrust his sword through the dead warrior. He spun around and slashed at the soldier behind him. He rolled under a swinging axe and kicked the owner over the edge of the ship. He turned around to see who was next.

Liz landed and immediately dodged to the side. She swung her broadsword around and took the head off the dead man in front of her. She stepped around a flying spear and slew another warrior. She parried a sword and thrust hers into the holder. She glanced around to see the deck was nearly clear of enemies and readied her sword as one ran towards her. She hesitated, only for a moment, recognizing the face behind the sword. She cleared her head as the soldier reached her, swinging her sword forward.

Vrisatore and Rinatore tore through the dead soldiers around them. They had fought battles side by side against enemies such as these many times before and this was no different. A circle was forming around them as they killed anyone who stepped forward. But these were dead people. They knew no fear. They knew only how to kill. But in that, they did not succeed. The two Slayers looked over at the other ship as the last enemy crumbled to dust at their feet. Both ships were now free of fighting.

They looked back and saw more ships approaching but they didn't have the time to get off these ships and onto the others. The catapult continued firing, as did the archers. Just then, Alex heard a cheer go up from behind him. He looked back to see ships coming around the fort, the flag of Livona flying above them.

Both groups took the emergency boats and rowed ashore swiftly. They had only lost three warriors in the battle. From there, they turned back and watched the two fleets engage in a sea battle. It was too dangerous to shoot catapults now. They all gathered together with Captain Graham as the troops celebrated their victory.

"My Gods, that was quick!" exclaimed Alex once they were all safely ashore.

"Aye, it was," said Vrisatore. "As I said, it was only a small force to draw us off and tire us out."

"Those dead people will be a problem," said Liz. "They unsettle the troops, especially as we may know some of them. They are good fighters."

"Yes, they are," said Alex. "But that is a problem for another day. Tonight, we rest and tomorrow we head back. We must return as swiftly as possible."

"Yes, we should." Liz smiled over at him. "But let's relax while we can."

They headed back towards their camp, with the soldiers following behind. The final dead ship sank beneath the waves and the duchy crews brought their boats ashore.

When they were three days away from Cosando and had just finished setting up camp for the night, Alex fell silent as two troops walked towards him, escorting an old man, hobbling along between them. The soldiers saluted as they approached.

"My Lord Duke, we were on guard and we saw this old man passing," began one of them. "We asked him his business and he said he had information for the duke. We thought we should bring him to you, sir."

"Thank you. I'll talk to him," said Alex. The men saluted and left. "You have information for the duke?"

"I have walked a long way, from the path I did stray," said the old man.

He had a long cloak pulled around him, casting a shadow over his face. He was slouched over. Vrisatore seemed startled from his thoughts and looked at the figure.

"Well, then tell me. I am the Duke of this land. What have you to say?"

"The enemy army is ready - they are on the way already."

The people around the fire began muttering between themselves. Vrisatore was still staring at the old man.

"Master Primatore? You are here?" asked Vrisatore suddenly.

The man straightened up. The cloak dropped away, revealing an elegant face and white hair flowing to his shoulders. The elf was grinning. At his side were two swords, the hilts cracked. Vrisatore and Rinatore hurriedly got to their feet and bowed low, right hands placed reverently on their chests.

"My Master, it has been so long," said Vrisatore. "Why are you here?"

"This planet was peaceful, the mountains were blissful."

"You know him?" asked Alex, looking back and forth between them. "Who is he?"

"He can explain," said Vrisatore.

Primatore cleared his throat and began.

"I am The First, the one who was cursed.

I am The Lyrical Lord, wielder of a broken sword.

I am The Wanderer, the fear of any conqueror.

I am Primatore, whose time is no more."

"When will this army arrive?" asked Alex, turning back to the important matter.

"In around a fortnight, they'll arrive with all their might. Now I must go, I have said all I know." Primatore picked up his cloak and turned to leave.

"Master, why don't you stay?" asked Vrisatore. "We could use your skill."

"Those days are done, I've had my fun," he said over his shoulder.

"Where will you go, Master?"

"I will wander the Universe, the stars I will traverse. It is what I always do, now good luck to you."

With that, he disappeared into the night, leaving everyone sitting around the fire, still dazed by what they had just witnessed.

"Who was that?" asked Alex after a while.

Vrisatore stirred from his thoughts and looked across the fire at him.

"He was the greatest Slayer to ever travel the Universe. The High Priest told you about the Ancients. Well, he was the first Ancient. And my Master."

"He is an elf too?" asked Alex.

Vrisatore nodded.

"Why did he stop if he was so great?"

"Thousands upon thousands of years ago, just after I finished my apprenticeship, he was captured by the Abominable Power himself. The darkness knew he was the best of us. For years he was tortured. Most people die or give in when they are tortured, not Primatore. He would sing the whole time he was captured to annoy his guards. Eventually, the Darkness became so angry, it cursed him to always speak in rhyme. Ultimately, the Slayers for the Sky made an attempt to rescue him. We succeeded. But he didn't want to go back to fighting. His sword had been broken. He disappeared and was rarely seen again. However, he seems to know where and when dark minions will appear. Often it is reported that he is seen when Slayers are fighting minions."

"He is famous to all Slayers," said Rinatore. "All trainees are told stories about him."

"Can we trust this information he brings?" asked Alex.

"Definitely," said Vrisatore.

"Tell us of your apprenticeship, Vrisatore."

"It was a long time ago. The minion I had to kill was called Peneburk the Ferryman. He was once a wizard before he decided to follow the Darkness…"

***

Peneburk would travel to a planet and find a river that wasn't crossed much, one that had no bridge. Then he started spreading rumours that a horrible monster lived on the other side of the river, that only the greatest warrior could kill it. Heroes came from across the planet to fight the monster and the only way across was on the Ferryman's boat. When they got on board, he killed them before they reached the other side. Once all the heroes were killed, Peneburk would take over the planet.

Vrisatore was hunting this minion, though he didn't know this information at the time. He didn't even know the minion's name. He was just going from destroyed planet to destroyed planet, trying to find any trace of who or what the minion was. His Master, Primatore the First, went with him on this hunt.

One day, they landed on a planet. Rumours had already spread to the town they stopped in about a monster on the other side of a river. The two Slayers made ready to hunt down this monster. But before they could, another Slayer arrived on the planet. He brought a message from the Lord of the Sky, requesting for Primatore to go to him to help with an important matter. Primatore was the greatest Slayer there was and so his expertise was often required by the Gods.

Primatore left, instructing Vrisatore to do nothing until he returned. Vrisatore waited three days before deciding to go on by himself. He arrived late at night, travelling as fast as he could. He felt excited now, he had spent a lifetime preparing for this. The locals had told him how to get to the river. He had memorized the map, following it now as he approached the river. He knew he was getting close. There was the final hill, and then the boat on the river. The rain poured down around him. A pack of wild dogs howled in the distance. He approached the waiting boat, wary. He knew too many men had failed in killing this monster before. He got on board the boat, knowing there was no turning back now.

He looked at the old man at the oar. The Ferryman was cloaked, his face covered. He made his way slowly across the river. Lightning flashed and thunder rolled along the river. Then the Ferryman turned to him. Even from beneath the hood, Vrisatore could feel the force of the gaze. He shivered.

"What do you want?" he asked, angered.

"Everything," the Ferryman replied. Vrisatore sat confused for a moment, but in a flash of insight, he realised that the Ferryman was the minion he was hunting.

He drew his sword, making a swing at the cloaked figure. Suddenly, a staff blocked his sword. The rudder had transformed while he swung. The Ferryman laughed. The cloak dropped away from his shoulders, revealing an old, wizened face, a grey beard covering it. The entirety of the eyes glowed bright blue. 'So, a Slayer finally catches up with me,' he said, still chuckling. 'It took you long enough. And you, you are still an Apprentice. That is all they think to send after me? Well, you must die now. I am the powerful Peneburk, and I don't plan on surrendering.' Vrisatore stood his ground. 'No, you will die now. For too long have you wandered the Universe, killing whole planets. Now you will face justice.' But the Ferryman just laughed and began attacking.

For a long time, the two fought as the boat rocked beneath them. The Ferryman even cast a few spells. Eventually, Vrisatore spun his double-bladed sword around and sliced the Ferryman's staff in half. The Ferryman looked up in shock and with a final thrust, the minion died. Vrisatore panted, out of breath. He looked at the shore opposite, where he had left from and saw Primatore sitting there, sharpening his blade. His blade never needed to be sharpened, as it was made by the Gods but he sharpened it anyway. Around him lay piles of corpses of hideous creatures. He looked at Vrisatore and smiled. He had watched the whole fight and had stopped the Ferryman's creatures from interrupting.

***

"And so on that day, I became a Master, taking the name Penadoon. And I have travelled the Universe since then, hunting minion."

After Vrisatore fell silent, Alex sat gazing at the fire as if contemplating the story. Then suddenly roused himself to action.

"We must make all haste back," he said. "Primatore seemed to imply that this was the big army itself. We must travel fast. We shall leave at first light, so get some rest now." He stood and left the fire, heading for his tent.

16: The Battle

Alexander looked around the room. All of the other six dukes and the duchess were present, as well as the Slayers and some other officials. They had met in the throne room because the war room was too small for such a large gathering. They expected the battle to begin within the next day. All the armies of the duchies had gathered in front of Cosando City.

"So, friends, you all know why we are here," said Alex. "The army will reach us tomorrow. Are your troops ready?"

"Yes, mine are," said Duke Richard of Sirona. The others nodded. "But what is the plan for the battle?"

"It is simple, Richard. We engage their army while the Slayers here go around and kill Diabolous."

"Can't we just charge them down, surround them, and kill them all?" asked Duke George of Pomeria.

"No, George, we have been through this. The army is stronger than ours and fiercer. Doing it your way would get us all killed. No, we must kill the Master."

"What about the dead warriors? Won't they freak out our soldiers?" asked Duchess Victoria of Livona.

"Our soldiers have been warned, haven't they? All we can do is train them not to panic when they see them."

"Our whole plan is based on the word of these Slayers," said Duke Andrew of Cornalia. "Can we even trust them? Do we really know them?"

"What would you suggest, Andrew?" asked Duke Frederick of Tharingia. "Do you have any other ideas? No, I didn't think so. We should listen to these Slayers and stick to Alexander's plan."

"Are there any further questions?" asked Alex. The others shook their heads. "Good. Remember, we have an advantage. This is our land and we can prepare it as we like. Catapults have been built. We will use these to attack from a distance, reducing the size of their army. We cannot fail here tomorrow. If we do, the duchies are over. This is our last chance. Good luck."

Suddenly, Alex heard a commotion outside. The doors opened and a group of warriors entered the room. They bowed before the dukes, then their leader stepped forward.

"I am Kenair, leader of the troops from the Islands of Hostiban, sir," he said. All the warriors behind him had swords on their belts and their chests covered in tattoos. "King Kanakore sent us."

"We can't trust them!" Duke George burst out. "They are barbarians!"

"We need all the troops we can get," Duke Frederick said. "Let bygones be bygones, I say. They come here in friendship, to aid us. I say we let them."

"Yes, I agree with Duke Frederick," Alex said. "Do you bring many troops, Kenair?"

"Three thousand of our best, sir. They will not fail you."

"Good. This affects you as much as us. If that is all, I say you can go prepare your troops." He nodded at them and the dukes and the Islanders turned and left.

"Will this work?" Alex asked the Slayers after the others had left.

"Hopefully," said Vrisatore, shrugging. "It is the only way that we stand a chance. We have done all we can. Now, we wait."

"Where will you two-" he heard a growl and altered his question. "sorry, three, go to?"

"We will wait for nightfall and creep around the back of the army. Diabolous doesn't lead from the front. He prefers to follow behind. So that's where we will be."

"Well, good luck, then." They shook hands. "I hope you succeed."

"So do we, Duke. So do we."

The Slayers turned and left the room, with Rumdam the tiger getting up and stretching before following them out.

***

Alex hurried down to his chamber. Horns were sounding out all across the city and the soldiers' camps. The enemy was here.

Alex arrived at his room and threw on his armour. He grabbed his sword and shield from their place on the wall. He swiftly left the palace, mounting his horse to get to the front line quicker. He arrived to see the troops gathering together, preparing for the oncoming army. Alex dismounted and headed towards the Cosando soldiers. He passed Elizabeth on his way. She was going towards the Mirando troops. She stopped when she saw him.

"Good luck," Alex said as they hugged. "Give 'em hell."

"Don't die," she whispered into his ear, kissed him on the cheek, before letting go. She hurried away without looking back.

Alex reached the front and found General Edward waiting for him. They shook hands.

"Are the soldiers ready?" asked Alex.

"Yes, Your Grace. Ready and waiting."

"Good." Alex turned to his men and raised his voice.

"Soldiers! Today we fight! Today we kill these monsters that think they can take over our land! They have killed thousands of people and destroyed many countries! Well, today it stops! We will teach them to fear mankind! To fear the duchies! We fight today for everything! For our families! For our friends! For those who died for this cause! For our land! For Cosando!"

"FOR COSANDO!" the troops shouted back.

Alex turned back and surveyed the landscape for any sign of the enemy army. In the distance, he saw goblins getting ready, climbing onto their cougars. Then they began running. Alex looked overhead to see the catapults shoot their first load. They crashed among the riding goblins and some among the foot soldiers behind. The archers around Alex readied their bows and began firing.

Alex raised his shield as the enemy cavalry arrived. He had a spear by his side and he thrust it forward. The first cougar fell over, dragging the spear from his hand. Alex drew his sword and stabbed the goblin rider. He blocked another flying sword and a wild swing of his own dug deep into a cougar's skin. The first wave was over quickly.

He looked ahead at more goblins approaching, their loping strides bringing them ever closer. Soldiers stepped up beside him to replace those that had died fighting the cougars. The goblin horde hit and Alex fought wildly, slicing, dodging, blocking. Many goblins fell before his blade. Soldiers around him died and were replaced and still he fought on. Scattered among the goblin horde were riderless cougars, clawing at any soldier that approached. Then the dead arrived. They were better fighters than the goblins, more precise. They made none of the mistakes the goblins made out of greed. The dead don't feel anything. Suddenly, in front of Alex, a space cleared. Walking towards him was Bruce.

Vrisatore looked out from behind the rock. He could see Diabolous striding along, his back turned to them. Five officer goblins surrounded him. Vrisatore looked over at Rinatore. Rinatore nodded at him. They both silently pulled out their weapons. One last look and then they leapt out from behind their cover. A short sprint across open ground and they were on the goblins. The goblins spotted them too late. Vrisatore took down two of them immediately, using both blades of his sword. Rinatore took the head off the nearest one. Rumdam killed the fourth one easily, tearing his teeth through its throat. The last officer had more time and made a futile swing at Vrisatore. Vrisatore stopped the moving spear with one blade and brought the other side around into the goblin's stomach. Then they turned to face Diabolous.

Diabolous stared back at them. He hadn't moved at all during the fight. His helmet was in his hand. He smiled as they circled him.

"Well, well, well. You have finally caught up with me," he said. "I'll admit, I thought you would take a little longer to find this planet. I had hoped to have it finished before you got here. Oh, well. I'll just kill you and get on with it." He nodded his head at something they couldn't see while he put on his helmet.

Abruptly, a cougar came flying from behind them and tackled Rumdam. It was fully white and much bigger than all the other cougars. The two great cats launched into a vicious fight, rolling across the ground, then straightening up, circling each other, jumping together, biting and clawing when they got the chance.

Vrisatore turned back to Diabolous just as a spear came swinging towards him. He blocked it and swung his sword around. It clashed against the armour, leaving a dent. Diabolous pushed him to the ground and turned to block a swing from Rinatore. He thrust his spear and it crashed into Rinatore's shield. Diabolous' fist came around and sent Rinatore sprawling back against a rock. Vrisatore saw Rinatore's head droop onto his chest as he stood up again. He turned back to face Diabolous.

Meanwhile, Alex faced a terror of his own.

"Bruce?" he said, his sword dropping to his side. "What are you doing here?"

Bruce smiled wickedly, two swords at his side dripping blood. Suddenly, he leapt forward. Alex managed to raise his shield in time and both swords smashed into it. Bruce backed off slightly and began to circle Alex. Around them the battle still raged but a space had cleared around the brothers.

"Oh, no. I can't believe you died," said Alex. "But this isn't you. You can fight this. You don't have to serve him. Together, we can fight this."

Alex was ignoring all he had told others about the dead. He had told them to kill them without hesitation, as they weren't real. *But Bruce is different,* thought Alex. *He must be. He is my brother. There must be a way.*

Bruce was still grinning. He launched forward into another attack. Alex was forced to retreat backwards under the rain of blows. He blocked and he parried but he did not go on the attack. He swung no hits of his own. Bruce stopped again and continued circling.

"I won't fight you, Bruce. I refuse to succumb to his tricks. He is evil. We won't do what he wants. We must resist."

"You're weak," Bruce growled. His voice had changed. It was the only part of him which had changed at all. "The Master can make us strong. He made me strong. I serve Him faithfully now. He freed me. He is powerful. More powerful than you or any mortal could ever be. And He wants you dead. So you will be dead."

"Please, Bruce. I know you. You can resist."

Bruce shrugged and began attacking again while Alex was off guard. Alex raised his shield and caught the blade. He heard the shield crack and splinter apart as Bruce withdrew his sword. Alex threw aside what was left of his shield and gripped his sword with both hands. Bruce swung, Alex parried. Bruce swung, Alex parried. Again and again.

Suddenly, Bruce took a step back. Alex dropped his guard slightly, only to see one of Bruce's swords flying towards him. It caught him on the shoulder. He spun around and fell to the floor, his sword clattering against a rock. He quickly began crawling backwards. Bruce leant down, picked up the sword and started walking forward, a grin spreading across his face. He lifted one sword over his head. Alex raised his hands in front of his face, knowing it would do nothing to stop what was coming.

"Humans," said Diabolous, laughing, as he turned to face Vrisatore. "Always so weak. And yet so sure of themselves. They are the worst race, am I not right, Master Vrisatore?"

"You will die, Diabolous. For too long have you wandered the Universe, killing whole planets. Now you will face justice."

"Maybe," Diabolous grew serious. "But it won't change. Another will take my place. You cannot win. The Darkness is always there and will always be there. You may win today. But we will take the Universe eventually."

Vrisatore could see the glow of his eyes through the helmet as he spoke.

Vrisatore leapt forward and brought his sword down onto Diabolous. Diabolous swung his spear around and caught Vrisatore on the shoulder. He recovered quickly and brought his sword down onto Diabolous' foot. As he bent over, Vrisatore brought his sword around and caught the edge of Diabolous' helmet. It flew away. Diabolous straightened up, a mad glint in his eye. No-one had ever done so much damage before. Vrisatore made another swing but the spear blocked it. Another swing, another block. Diabolous brought his foot up and kicked Vrisatore backwards. His sword slipped from his hand.

Diabolous raised his spear high, ready for a final thrust. Suddenly, he reared back, a flash of orange landing on his back. Diabolous reached back, grabbed Rumdam and flung him away. Cuts covered the tiger's fur, a tribute to his recent fight. The white cougar lay on its side, its fur more red than white as blood poured from its wounds.

Diabolous turned back to Vrisatore but he'd vanished. He glanced around and just saw him in time to raise his spear. They clashed together. Vrisatore rained blow after blow down onto the spear, Diabolous retreating backwards. With a powerful blow, Vrisatore severed one end of the spear. He swung his blade around and with one final thrust stabbed Diabolous. The point was so sharp and the thrust so strong it went right through the armour.

Diabolous let out a scream. His power slowly drained. He fell forward. As he fell, he reverted to his true shape. Gone was the elegant face and the massive height. In its place, a hideous creature, scars covering its face so much you could barely make out the features. He was smaller than a regular man. He was still screaming.

Alex looked into his brother's face as the sword bore down on him. He could see the lack of thought in his eyes. Only malice and the need for violence. A scream cut through his thoughts, ringing across the battlefield. The look changed in Bruce's eyes. Understanding dawned on him. His swords clattered to the ground.

Alex scrambled to his feet. He caught Bruce as he fell to the floor. Bruce looked into his eyes, recognized him and smiled.

"Finally," he said. "Finally. Freedom."

Alex let out a sob.

"Don't cry, Al. I go now to Helena. And to rest."

He crumbled to dust in Alex's arms.

Alex looked through his tears at the battlefield. The screaming had stopped. The goblins were fleeing, their Master gone. Most didn't get far before they were killed. Everywhere, the dead warriors were slowly disappearing. Later, Alex reflected that this was probably because the Master's power was draining slowly, rather than all at once when the dead were stabbed.

"Alex!"

Liz came running towards him. He opened his arms and she fell into them. They hugged, then he leant down and kissed her.

"You're okay?" she asked, tears of joy streaming down her face.

"Yeah, yeah, I'm fine," he said, wiping away his own tears. He winced. "Just a cut in my shoulder. I'm so glad to see you are okay."

They stood there like that for a moment, in each other's arms. Then Alex let go.

"Come on," he said, smiling. "Let's find Vrisatore."

They found Vrisatore helping Rinatore up from the ground. Beside them was a hideous looking body, pieces of spear and armour lying around it. Vrisatore smiled when he saw them. Both Slayers looked a bit bruised but nothing serious. They seemed weary more than anything else.

"You two injured?" asked Vrisatore.

"Nah, we're fine," said Alex, his arm around Liz.

"That's good, that's good."

"Is it over? Have we won?" asked Liz.

Vrisatore nodded.

"Not yet," a voice snarled. Behind him, the creature Diabolous had become reared up. Before they could react, he leapt forward and stuck the point of a spear into Vrisatore. Rinatore swung his sword and the head of Diabolous left its body. He crumpled to the floor, as did Vrisatore.

"No, no, no," cried Rinatore, kneeling beside his Master.

Rumdam got up from where he had been lying and crawled next to Vrisatore. Vrisatore smiled wanly and rubbed Rumdam's blood-soaked fur. Rinatore was trying to patch up the wound but Vrisatore forced his hands away.

"Don't. It's too late," he coughed slightly. "Rinatore, you have slain Diabolous. You have finished your Apprenticeship. I proclaim you Rinatore Diabadoon, Master Slayer for the Land. Good luck."

Vrisatore lay back and closed his eyes. Rumdam let out a low whine as they both died together, side by side.

Alex and Liz looked on transfixed, as the bodies disappeared. A moment later, an eagle soared up from where they had lain, hovered above them for a moment before flying towards the mountains.

"What was that?" asked Alex.

Rinatore stood up.

"The gift of all Slayers," he replied, wiping his tears. "In return for our years of service, after we die, we take on another life as a creature for the division we follow."

Together, they looked out across the battlefield, where the clean up was already beginning. The goblins who had headed for the mountains had run straight into a force of soldiers, wearing the Empire's colours, who slew them all.

***

Alex looked up as Rinatore entered the throne room. A week had passed since the great battle. After the death of Diabolous, a sense of joy had engulfed the city of Cosando but the joy was matched by sorrow. Many soldiers had died fighting the goblins and the dead and they had all been buried in great mounds. Alex had ordered a statue to be built for them so that their sacrifice would never be forgotten.

After the battle, the dukes had left and taken most of their armies with them. Kenair led his Islanders home, taking prospects of new trade deals with them. Liz stayed behind with Alex, who still bore the scar down his shoulder where his brother's blade had cut him. He sent squads of soldiers to hunt down any goblins that had escaped. He couldn't risk the possibility that they might regroup. Not many goblins did escape. Alex met up with the soldiers from the Empire afterwards and they told how they had killed most of the fleeing goblins. The soldiers introduced themselves as 'The Legacy'.

"Alex, I'm afraid I must leave you now," said Rinatore.

"So soon?" asked Alex. He would be sad to see him go. They had grown close in the days after the battle. "Why not stay for a while? We would be glad to have your company."

"Alas, it is my time to leave. I must report to my Lord and return the sword of Vrisatore. They must know of his death and I have an obligation to take on a new mission."

"Then please take this, as a token of our thanks."

Alex nodded to one of the servants, who stepped forward with a necklace.

"This is the Pendant of Aurune. It has been in my family for generations. You have earned it, for ridding us of that monster."

Rinatore received the necklace and bowed.

"I thank you, Duke Alexander. It has been an honour meeting you. I wish you good fortune. To you as well, Lady Elizabeth."

She smiled back at him from her place beside the throne.

"May your travels go well," she said.

He nodded at both of them again before leaving. As he left, he passed the leader of The Legacy walking in. They nodded at each other.

"William, how goes the search?" asked Alex.

"Very good, sir. We have hunted down most of the surviving gangs. They won't last much longer."

"That's good. Now, I have some good news for you." Alex picked up a letter that had been lying beside him. "This came earlier on from Marthor, the island city off the west coast of the Empire. It says that it and many of the other islands formerly of the Empire have been able to survive and withstand attacks. They are planning on rebuilding what they can."

"That is indeed great news, sir." Alex could see the joy in his eyes. "With your permission, I will leave here and go to them with my warriors. They will need help rebuilding."

"Of course. Good luck to you."

William bowed again before hurrying out of the room.

"So many dead," said Alex sadly. "So many of the people I once knew, dead because of this war."

"I know," Liz said. "But things will change. We will rebuild and who knows? Maybe it will be even better than before."

"Maybe," Alex smiled at her.

Epilogue

As Rinatore approached, the doors swung open of their own accord. He strode through and knelt before Lord Thaddeus and Lady Tabitha of the Sky.

"My Lord and Lady, I return the sword of Vrisatore Penadoon, my Master who fell in battle," said Rinatore, holding up the sword in front of him.

Lord Thaddeus reached and took it.

"Vrisatore will be missed," said Lord Thaddeus, looking at the blade. "He was a good warrior."

"And a good man," said Lady Tabitha. "He helped many people in his long life. May his second life be good."

"Rise, Master Rinatore," said Lord Thaddeus. "We thank you for returning the sword. And congratulate you on slaying Diabolous. May he not be the last that you end. Now go. You must report to your own Lord and Lady, Lord Aegeus and Lady Axelia of the Land."

"May you live long and receive glory," said Lady Tabitha.

Rinatore stood up, bowed, and left.

"Another one fallen," said Lady Tabitha.

"I know. He had lived for a long time. He deserves his rest now."

Lord Thaddeus stood up and left the big throne room. Lady Tabitha followed him. They walked down the hallway and into the Hall of the Fallen. They strode over to a free space, a rack standing empty. Lord Thaddeus placed the sword on it. A servant came out, holding a sign in his hand. He bowed and handed it to the God. Thaddeus hung it over the sword. It read:

Master Vrisatore Penadoon,

Slayer for the Sky,

Apprentice of Primatore the First,

Died fighting.

The Lord and Lady stepped back and looked at it and then around the large hall, filled with similar signs. They both sighed, before leaving the room. They had to see to other tasks. There is a whole Universe to oversee when you're a God.

About the Author

Tim Callanan lives and writes in Cork, Ireland. He is an avid reader of science fiction and fantasy novels.

Inspired to begin writing during school lockdown in early 2020, Tim enjoys writing and creating worlds where the characters can sometimes surprise even him.

This, his first novel, *The Dead Shall March*, was completed on the eve of his sixteenth birthday.

Printed in Poland
by Amazon Fulfillment
Poland Sp. z o.o., Wrocław

62703081R00099